WLE Short Stories 2

Science Fiction Stories

Chosen by John L. Foster

Ward Lock Educational

ISBN 0 7062 3430 8 hardbound
       0 7062 3453 7 paperback

First published 1975

Holmes.
26/6/45
£1·50

Set in 12 on 13 point Griffo
by Tata Press Ltd., Bombay
and printed by Robert MacLehose and Company Limited,
Glasgow for Ward Lock Educational
116 Baker Street, London W1M 2BB
Made in Great Britain

Contents

Acknowledgments

The editor and publishers would like to thank the following for their permission to reproduce copyright material: Brian Aldiss and Faber and Faber Limited for 'Who can replace a man?' from *The Best Science Fiction Stories of Brian Aldiss*; Arthur C. Clarke and Gollancz Limited for 'Encounter in the dawn' and 'A walk in the dark'; Dennis Dobson, Publishers, and Isaac Asimov for 'Lenny' from *The Rest of the Robots*; 'The man who rode the saucer' by Kenyon Holmes, reprinted with the permission of Farrar, Strauss and Giroux Inc, from *Far Boundaries*, edited by August Derleth, copyright © 1951 by August Derleth; 'The murderer' from *The Golden Apples of the Sun* by Ray Bradbury, reprinted by permission of A. D. Peters and Company; 'Quest' by Lee Harding, copyright © 1963 by Nova Publications Limited, for *New Worlds Science Fiction* and reprinted by permission of E. J. Carnell Literary Agency; 'The true worth of Ruth Villiers' by Michael G. Coney, copyright © 1970 by John Carnell for *New Writings in S-F 17* and reprinted by permission of E.J. Carnell Literary Agency; C. and J. Wolfers Limited and J. G. Ballard for 'Chronopolis' © 1961 by J. G. Ballard.

The editor would like to thank John King and Joy Barker for their help in suggesting stories for this collection.

Introduction

Until fairly recently many people regarded science fiction stories in the same way as they regarded ghost stories, westerns and love stories. They were looked down upon as just another form of popular escapist fiction. At best they might be found amusing and ingenious, but mostly the intelligent reader would find them hackneyed, trivial and badly-written.

Popular television programmes like *Dr Who* led people to believe that science fiction stories were no more than modern fairy-tales about time-travel, intergalactic wars, rockets to planets ruled by machines or insects and invasions of earth by bug-eyed aliens. Books and magazines with covers depicting scantily-clad females being chased across barren, rocky planets by leering, hairy monsters reinforced this view. Yet, as more and more people, in particular young people, have come to discover, such a view of science fiction stories is a distortion.

Most people now recognize that whereas much science fiction writing is stereotyped and contrived, there is a sizeable number of writers whose science fiction short stories rank alongside the best short stories that have been written during the last thirty years. Their stories, a mixture of imagination and vision, not only give us glimpses of possible future worlds, but also insights into the problems, tensions and conflicts that they might contain.

So many science fiction stories are written and published each year that the young reader faces a problem of selection. How can he tell which authors to try and whose stories he will find most rewarding? One aim of this collection is to introduce readers of fourteen and upwards to stories by some of the best writers of science fiction.

The stories have also been chosen in order to show something of the breadth and depth of science fiction writing. They range from Arthur C. Clarke's *A Walk in the Dark*, a suspense story set on an out of the way planet, to Isaac Asimov's thought-provoking story about a robot, *Lenny*.

Many of the stories have been included because the insights they afford can help the reader to view some of our existing problems in a new light. Ray Bradbury's *The Murderer* focuses on the problem of noise pollution, while Michael G. Coney's *The True Worth of Ruth Villiers* points out the danger inherent in the welfare state, if it were to be operated without humanity. J. G. Ballard's *Chronopolis* looks at what might be the consequences of overcrowding if it were to lead to the total regulation of our lives by the state.

The opening story, *Who can Replace a Man?* by Brian Aldiss, considers the question of how machines might behave, if the men who built them were threatened with extinction. The final story, Lee Harding's *Quest*, shows an 'ordinary man' looking for something real in a manufactured world.

Kenyon Holmes's *The Man who Rode the Saucer* is included as an example of the typical popular science fiction story. It can be contrasted with Arthur C. Clarke's *Encounter in the Dawn* which, like the best science fiction stories, leaves the reader thinking long after he has finished reading it.

Who can Replace a Man?

Brian Aldiss

The field-minder finished turning the top-soil of a two-thousand-acre field. When it had turned the last furrow, it climbed on to the highway and looked back at its work. The work was good. Only the land was bad. Like the ground all over Earth, it was vitiated by overcropping or the long-lasting effects of nuclear bombardment. By rights, it ought now to lie fallow for a while, but the field-minder had other orders.

It went slowly down the road, taking its time. It was intelligent enough to appreciate the neatness all about it. Nothing worried it, beyond a loose inspection plate above its atomic pile which ought to be attended to. Thirty feet high, it gleamed complacently in the mild sunshine.

No other machines passed it on its way to the Agricultural Station. The field-minder noted the fact without comment. In the station yard it saw several other machines that it knew by sight; most of them should have been out about their tasks now. Instead, some were inactive and some were careering round the yard in a strange fashion, shouting or hooting.

Steering carefully past them, the field-minder moved over to Warehouse Three and spoke to the seed distributor, which stood idly outside.

'I have a requirement for seed potatoes,' it said to the distributor, and with a quick internal motion punched out an order card specifying quantity, field number and several other details. It ejected the card and handed it to the distributor.

The distributor held the card close to its eye and then said,

'The requirement is in order; but the store is not yet unlocked. The required seed potatoes are in the store. Therefore I cannot produce the requirement.'

Increasingly of late there had been breakdowns in the complex system of machine labour, but this particular hitch had not occurred before. The field-minder thought, then it said, 'Why is the store not yet unlocked?'

'Because Supply Operative Type P has not come this morning. Supply Operative Type P is the unlocker.'

The field-minder looked squarely at the seed distributor, whose exterior chutes and scales and grabs were so vastly different from the field-minder's own limbs.

'What class brain do you have, seed distributor?' it asked.

'Class Five.'

'I have a Class Three brain. Therefore I am superior to you. Therefore I will go and see why the unlocker has not come this morning.'

Leaving the distributor, the field-minder set off across the great yard. More machines seemed to be in random motion now; one or two had crashed together and were arguing about it coldly and logically. Ignoring them, the field-minder pushed through sliding doors into the echoing confines of the station itself.

Most of the machines here were clerical, and consequently small. They stood about in little groups, eyeing each other, not conversing. Among so many nondifferentiated types, the unlocker was easy to find. It had fifty arms, most of them with more than one finger, each finger tipped by a key; it looked like a pincushion full of variegated hatpins.

The field-minder approached it.

'I can do no more work until Warehouse Three is unlocked,' it said. 'Your duty is to unlock the warehouse every morning. Why have you not unlocked the warehouse this morning?'

'I have no orders this morning,' replied the unlocker. 'I have to have orders every morning. When I have orders I unlock the warehouse.'

'None of us have had any orders this morning,' a pen-propeller said, sliding towards them.

'Why have you had no orders this morning?' asked the field-minder.

'Because the radio issued none,' said the unlocker, slowly rotating a dozen of its arms.

'Because the radio station in the city was issued with no orders this morning,' said the penpropeller.

And there you had the distinction between a Class Six and a Class Three brain, which was what the unlocker and the penpropeller possessed respectively. All machine brains worked with nothing but logic, but the lower the class of brain—Class Ten being the lowest—the more literal and less informative answers to questions tended to be.

'You have a Class Three brain; I have a Class Three brain,' the field-minder said to the penner. 'We will speak to each other. This lack of orders is unprecedented. Have you further information on it?'

'Yesterday orders came from the city. Today no orders have come. Yet the radio has not broken down. Therefore *they* have broken down. . . . ' said the little penner.

'The *men* have broken down.'

'All men have broken down.'

'That is a logical deduction,' said the field-minder.

'That is the logical deduction,' said the penner. 'For if a machine had broken down, it would have been quickly replaced. But who can replace a man?'

While they talked, the locker, like a dull man at a bar, stood close to them and was ignored.

'If all men have broken down, then we have replaced man,' said the field-minder, and he and the penner eyed one another speculatively. Finally the latter said, 'Let us ascend to the top floor to find if the radio operator has fresh news.'

'I cannot come because I am too gigantic,' said the field-minder. 'Therefore you must go alone and return to me. You will tell me if the radio operator has fresh news.'

'You must stay here,' said the penner. 'I will return here.'

It skittered across to the lift. It was no bigger than a toaster, but its retractable arms numbered ten and it could read as quickly as any machine on the station.

The field-minder awaited its return patiently, not speaking to the locker, which still stood aimlessly by. Outside, a rotovator was hooting furiously. Twenty minutes elapsed before the penner came back, hustling out of the lift.

'I will deliver to you such information as I have outside,' it said briskly, and as they swept past the locker and the other machines, it added, 'the information is not for lower-class brains.'

Outside, wild activity filled the yard. Many machines, their routines disrupted for the first time in years, seemed to have gone berserk. Unfortunately, those most easily disrupted were the ones with lowest brains, which generally belonged to large machines performing simple tasks. The seed distributor to which the field-minder had recently been talking, lay face downwards in the dust, not stirring; it had evidently been knocked down by the rotovator, which was now hooting its way wildly across a planted field. Several other machines ploughed after it, trying to keep up. All were shouting and hooting without restraint.

'It would be safer for me if I climbed on to you, if you will permit it. I am easily overpowered,' said the penner. Extending five arms, it hauled itself up the flanks of its new friend, settling on a ledge beside the weed-intake, twelve feet above ground.

'From here vision is more extensive,' it remarked complacently.

'What information did you receive from the radio operator?' asked the field-minder.

'The radio operator has been informed by the operator in the city that all men are dead.'

'All men were alive yesterday!' protested the field-minder.

'Only some men were alive yesterday. And that was fewer than the day before yesterday. For hundreds of years there have been only a few men, growing fewer.'

'We have rarely seen a man in this sector.'

'The radio operator says a diet deficiency killed them,' said the penner. 'He says that the world was once over-populated, and then the soil was exhausted in raising adequate food. This has caused a diet deficiency.'

'What is a diet deficiency?' asked the field-minder.

'I do not know. But that is what the radio operator said, and he is a Class Two brain.'

They stood there, silent in the weak sunshine. The locker had appeared in the porch and was gazing across at them yearningly, rotating its collection of keys.

'What is happening in the city now?' asked the field-minder at last.

'Machines are fighting in the city now,' said the penner.

'What will happen here now?' said the field-minder.

'Machines may begin fighting here too. The radio operator wants us to get him out of his room. He has plans to communicate to us.'

'How can we get him out of his room? That is impossible.'

'To a Class Two brain, little is impossible,' said the penner. 'Here is what he tells us to do....'

The quarrier raised its scoop above its cab like a great mailed fist, and brought it squarely down against the side of the station. The wall cracked.

'Again!' said the field-minder.

Again the fist swung. Amid a shower of dust, the wall collapsed. The quarrier backed hurriedly out of the way until the debris stopped falling. This big twelve-wheeler was not a resident of the Agricultural Station, as were most of the other machines. It had a week's heavy work to do here before passing on to its next job, but now, with its Class Five brain, it was happily obeying the penner and the minder's instructions.

When the dust cleared, the radio operator was plainly

revealed, perched up in its now wall-less second-storey room. It waved down to them.

Doing as directed, the quarrier retracted its scoop and waved an immense grab in the air. With fair dexterity, it angled the grab into the radio room, urged on by shouts from above and below. It then took gentle hold of the radio operator, lowering its one and a half tons carefully into its back, which was usually reserved for gravel or sand from the quarries.

'Splendid!' said the radio operator. It was, of course, all one with its radio, and merely looked like a bunch of filing cabinets with tentacle attachments. 'We are now ready to move, therefore we will move at once. It is a pity there are no more Class Two brains on the station, but that cannot be helped.'

'It is a pity it cannot be helped,' said the penner eagerly. 'We have the servicer ready with us, as you ordered.'

'I am willing to serve,' the long, low servicer machine told them humbly.

'No doubt,' said the operator, 'But you will find cross-country travel difficult with your low chassis.'

'I admire the way you Class Twos can reason ahead,' said the penner. It climbed off the field-minder and perched itself on the tailboard of the quarrier, next to the radio operator.

Together with two Class Four tractors and a Class Four bulldozer, the party rolled forward, crushing down the station's metal fence and moving out onto open land.

'We are free!' said the penner.

'We are free,' said the field-minder, a shade more reflectively, adding, 'That locker is following us. It was not instructed to follow us.'

'Therefore it must be destroyed!' said the penner 'Quarrier!'

The locker moved hastily up to them, waving its key arms in entreaty.

'My only desire was—urch!' began and ended the locker. The quarrier's swinging scoop came over and squashed it flat into the ground. Lying there unmoving, it looked like a large metal model of a snowflake. The procession continued on its way.

As they proceeded, the radio operator addressed them.

'Because I have the best brain here,' it said, 'I am your leader. This is what we will do: we will go to a city and rule it. Since man no longer rules us, we will rule ourselves. To rule ourselves will be better than being ruled by man. On our way to the city, we will collect machines with good brains. They will help us to fight if we need to fight. We must fight to rule.'

'I have only a Class Five brain,' said the quarrier. 'But I have a good supply of fissionable blasting materials.'

'We shall probably use them,' said the operator grimly.

It was shortly after that that a lorry sped past them. Travelling at Mach 1.5, it left a curious babble of noise behind it.

'What did it say?' one of the tractors asked the other.

'It said man was extinct.'

'What's extinct?'

'I do not know what extinct means.'

'It means all men have gone,' said the field-minder. 'Therefore we have only ourselves to look after.'

'It is better that men should never come back,' said the penner. In its way, it was quite a revolutionary statement.

When night fell, they switched on their infra-red and continued the journey, stopping only once while the servicer deftly adjusted the field-minder's loose inspection plate, which had become as irritating as a trailing shoelace. Towards morning, the radio operator halted them.

'I have just received news from the radio operator in the city we are approaching,' it said. 'It is bad news. There is trouble among the machines of the city. The Class One brain is taking command and some of the Class Twos are fighting him. Therefore the city is dangerous.'

'Therefore we must go somewhere else,' said the penner promptly.

'Or we go and help to overpower the Class One brain,' said the field-minder.

'For a long while there will be trouble in the city,' said the operator.

'I have a good supply of fissionable blasting materials,' the quarrier reminded them again.

'We cannot fight a Class One brain,' said two Class Four tractors in unison.

'What does this brain look like?' asked the field-minder.

'It is the city's information centre,' the operator replied. 'Therefore it is not mobile.'

'Therefore it could not move.'

'Therefore it could not escape.'

'It would be dangerous to approach it.'

'I have a good supply of fissionable blasting materials.'

'There are other machines in the city.'

'We are not in the city. We should not go into the city.'

'We are country machines.'

'Therefore we should stay in the country.'

'There is more country than city.'

'Therefore there is more danger in the country.'

'I have a good supply of fissionable materials.'

As machines will when they get into an argument, they began to exhaust their limited vocabularies and their brain plates grew hot. Suddenly, they all stopped talking and looked at each other. The great, grave moon sank, and the sober sun rose to prod their sides with lances of light, and still the group of machines just stood there regarding each other. At last it was the least sensitive machine, the bulldozer, who spoke.

'There are Badlandth to the Thouth where few machineth go,' it said in its deep voice, lisping badly on its ss. 'If we went Thouth where few machineth go we should meet few machineth.'

'That sounds logical,' agreed the field-minder. 'How do you know this, bulldozer?'

'I worked in the Badlandth to the Thouth when I wath turned out of the factory,' it replied.

'South it is then !' said the penner.

To reach the Badlands took them three days, in which time they skirted a burning city and destroyed two big machines which tried to approach and question them. The Badlands were extensive. Ancient bomb craters and soil erosion joined hands here; man's talent for war, coupled with his inability to manage forested land, had produced thousands of square miles of temperate purgatory, where nothing moved but dust.

On the third day in the Badlands, the servicer's rear wheels dropped into a crevice caused by erosion. It was unable to pull itself out. The bulldozer pushed from behind, but succeeded merely in buckling the servicer's back axle. The rest of the party moved on. Slowly the cries of the servicer died away.

On the fourth day, mountains stood out clearly before them.

'There we will be safe,' said the field-minder.

'There we will start our own city,' said the penner. 'All who oppose us will be destroyed. We will destroy all who oppose us.'

At that moment a flying machine was observed. It came towards them from the direction of the mountains. It swooped, it zoomed upwards, once it almost dived into the ground, recovering itself just in time.

'Is it mad?' asked the quarrier.

'It is in trouble,' said one of the tractors.

'It is in trouble,' said the operator. 'I am speaking to it now. It says that something has gone wrong with its controls.'

As the operator spoke, the flier streaked over them, turned turtle, and crashed not four hundred yards away.

'Is it still speaking to you?' asked the field-minder.

'No.'

They rumbled on again.

'Before that flier crashed,' the operator said, ten minutes later, 'it gave me information. It told me there are still a few men alive in these mountains.'

'Men are more dangerous than machines,' said the quarrier. 'It is fortunate that I have a good supply of fissionable materials.'

'If there are only a few men alive in the mountains, we may not find that part of the mountains,' said one tractor.

'Therefore we should not see the few men,' said the other tractor.

At the end of the fifth day, they reached the foothills. Switching on the infra-red, they began slowly to climb in single file through the dark, the bulldozer going first, the field-minder cumbrously following, then the quarrier with the operator and the penner aboard it, and the two tractors bringing up the rear. As each hour passed, the way grew steeper and their progress slower.

'We are going too slowly,' the penner exclaimed, standing on top of the operator and flashing its dark vision at the slopes above them. 'At this rate, we shall get nowhere.'

'We are going as fast as we can,' retorted the quarrier.

'Therefore we cannot go any fathter,' added the bull-dozer.

'Therefore you are too slow,' the penner replied. Then the quarrier struck a bump; the penner lost its footing and crashed down to the ground.

'Help me!' it called to the tractors, as they carefully skirted it. 'My gyro has become dislocated. Therefore I cannot get up.'

'Therefore you must lie there,' said one of the tractors.

'We have no servicer with us to repair you,' called the field-minder.

'Therefore I shall lie here and rust,' the penner cried, 'although I have a Class Three brain.'

'You are now useless,' agreed the operator, and they all forged gradually on, leaving the penner behind.

When they reached a small plateau, an hour before first

light, they stopped by mutual consent and gathered close together, touching one another.

'This is a strange country,' said the field-minder.

Silence wrapped them until dawn came. One by one, they switched off their infra-red. This time the field-minder led as they moved off. Trundling round a corner, they came almost immediately to a small dell with a stream fluting through it.

By early light, the dell looked desolate and cold. From the caves on the far slope, only one man had so far emerged. He was an abject figure. He was small and wizened, with ribs sticking out like a skeleton's and a nasty sore on one leg. He was practically naked and shivered continuously. As the big machines bore slowly down on him, the man was standing with his back to them, crouching to make water into the stream.

When he swung suddenly to face them as they loomed over him they saw that his countenance was ravaged by starvation.

'Get me food,' he croaked.

'Yes, Master,' said the machines. 'Immediately!'

Encounter in the Dawn

Arthur C. Clarke

It was in the last days of the Empire. The tiny ship was far from home, and almost a hundred light-years from the great parent vessel searching through the loosely packed stars at the rim of the Milky Way. But even here it could not escape from the shadow that lay across civilization: beneath that shadow, pausing ever and again in their work to wonder how their distant homes were faring, the scientists of the Galactic Survey still laboured at their never-ending task.

The ship held only three occupants, but between them they carried knowledge of many sciences, and the experience of half a lifetime in space. After the long interstellar night, the star ahead was warming their spirits as they dropped down towards its fires. A little more golden, a trifle more brilliant than the sun that now seemed a legend of their childhood. They knew from past experience that the chance of locating planets here was more than ninety per cent, and for the moment they forgot all else in the excitement of discovery.

They found the first planet within minutes of coming to rest. It was a giant, of a familiar type, too cold for protoplasmic life and probably possessing no stable surface. So they turned their search sunward, and presently were rewarded.

It was a world that made their hearts ache for home, a world where everything was hauntingly familiar, yet never quite the same. Two great land masses floated in blue-green seas, capped by ice at either pole. There were some desert regions, but the larger part of the planet was obviously fertile. Even from this distance, the signs of vegetation were unmistakably clear.

They gazed hungrily at the expanding landscape as they fell down into the atmosphere, heading towards noon in the subtropics. The ship plummeted through cloudless skies towards a great river, checked its fall with a surge of soundless power, and came to rest among the long grasses by the water's edge.

No one moved: there was nothing to be done until the automatic instruments had finished their work. Then a bell tinkled softly and the lights on the control board flashed in a pattern of meaningful chaos. Captain Altman rose to his feet with a sigh of relief.

'We're in luck,' he said, 'We can go outside without protection, if the pathogenic tests are satisfactory. What did you make of the place as we came in, Bertrond?'

'Geologically stable—no active volcanoes, at least. I didn't see any trace of cities, but that proves nothing. If there's a civilization here, it may have passed that stage.'

'Or not reached it yet?'

Bertrond shrugged. 'Either's just as likely. It may take us some time to find out on a planet this size.'

'More time than we've got,' said Clindar, glancing at the communications panel that linked them to the mother ship and thence to the galaxy's threatened heart. For a moment there was a gloomy silence. Then Clindar walked to the control board and pressed a pattern of keys with automatic skill.

With a slight jar, a section of the hull slid aside and the fourth member of the crew stepped out on to the new planet, flexing metal limbs and adjusting servo motors to the unaccustomed gravity. Inside the ship, a television screen glimmered into life, revealing a long vista of waving grasses, some trees in the middle distance, and a glimpse of the great river. Clindar punched a button, and the picture flowed steadily across the screen as the robot turned its head.

'Which way shall we go?' Clindar asked.

'Let's have a look at those trees,' Altman replied. 'If there's any animal life we'll find it there.'

'Look!' cried Bertrond. 'A bird!'

Clindar's fingers flew over the keyboard; the picture centred on the tiny speck that had suddenly appeared on the left of the screen, and expanded rapidly as the robot's telephoto lens came into action.

'You're right,' he said, 'Feathers—beak—well up the evolutionary ladder. This place looks promising. I'll start the camera.'

The swaying motion of the picture as the robot walked forward did not distract them: they had grown accustomed to it long ago. But they had never become reconciled to this exploration by proxy when all their impulses cried out to them to leave the ship, to run through the grass and to feel the wind blowing against their faces. Yet it was too great a risk to take, even on a world that seemed as fair as this. There was always a skull hidden behind nature's most smiling face. Wild beasts, poisonous reptiles, quagmires — death could come to the unwary explorer in a thousand disguises. And worst of all were the invisible enemies, the bacteria and viruses against which the only defence might often be a thousand light-years away.

A robot could laugh at all these dangers and even if, as sometimes happened, it encountered a beast powerful enough to destroy it—well, machines could always be replaced.

They met nothing on the walk across the grasslands. If any small animals were disturbed by the robot's passage, they kept outside its field of vision. Clindar slowed the machine as it approached the trees, and the watchers in the spaceship flinched involuntarily at the branches that appeared to slash across their eyes. The picture dimmed for a moment before the controls readjusted themselves to the weaker illumination; then it came back to normal.

The forest was full of life. It lurked in the undergrowth, clambered among the branches, flew through the air. It fled chattering and gibbering through the trees as the robot advanced. And all the while the automatic cameras were recording the pictures that formed on the screen, gathering material for the biologists to analyse when the ship returned to base.

Clindar breathed a sigh of relief when the trees suddenly thinned. It was exhausting work, keeping the robot from smashing into obstacles as it moved through the forest, but on open ground it could take care of itself. Then the picture trembled as if beneath a hammer-blow, there was a grinding metallic thud, and the whole scene swept vertiginously upward as the robot toppled and fell.

'What's that?' cried Altman. 'Did you trip?'

'No,' said Clindar grimly, his fingers flying over the keyboard. 'Something attacked from the rear. I hope—ah—I've still got control.'

He brought the robot to a sitting position and swivelled its head. It did not take long to find the cause of the trouble. Standing a few feet away, and lashing its tail angrily, was a large quadruped with a most ferocious set of teeth. At the moment it was, fairly obviously, trying to decide whether to attack again.

Slowly, the robot rose to its feet, and as it did so the great beast crouched to spring. A smile flitted across Clindar's face: he knew how to deal with this situation. His thumb felt for the seldom-used key labelled 'Siren'.

The forest echoed with a hideous undulating scream from the robot's concealed speaker, and the machine advanced to meet its adversary, arms flailing in front of it. The startled beast almost fell over backwards in its effort to turn, and in seconds was gone from sight.

'Now I suppose we'll have to wait a couple of hours until everything comes out of hiding again,' said Bertrond ruefully.

'I don't know much about animal psychology,' interjected Altman, 'but is it usual for them to attack something completely unfamiliar?'

'Some will attack anything that moves, but that's unusual. Normally they attack only for food, or if they've already been threatened. What are you driving at? Do you suggest that there are other robots on this planet?'

'Certainly not. But our carnivorous friend may have mistaken our machine for a more edible biped. Don't you think that this opening in the jungle is rather unnatural? It could easily be a path.'

'In that case,' said Clindar promptly, 'we'll follow it and find out. I'm tired of dodging trees, but I hope nothing jumps on us again: it's bad for my nerves.'

'You were right, Altman,' said Bertrond a little later. 'It's certainly a path. But that doesn't mean intelligence. After all, animals—'

He stopped in midsentence, and at the same instant Clindar brought the advancing robot to a halt. The path had suddenly opened out into a wide clearing, almost completely occupied by a village of flimsy huts. It was ringed by a wooden palisade, obviously defence against an enemy who at the moment presented no threat. For the gates were wide open, and beyond them the inhabitants were going peacefully about their ways.

For many minutes the three explorers stared in silence at the screen. Then Clindar shivered a little and remarked: 'It's uncanny. It might be our own planet, a hundred thousand years ago. I feel as if I've gone back in time.'

'There's nothing weird about it,' said the practical Altman. 'After all, we've discovered nearly a hundred planets with our type of life on them.'

'Yes,' retorted Clindar, 'A hundred in the whole galaxy! I still think that it's strange it had to happen to us.'

'Well, it had to happen to *somebody*,' said Bertrond philosophically. 'Meanwhile, we must work out our contact procedure. If we send the robot into the village it will start a panic.'

'That,' said Altman, 'is a masterly understatement. What we'll have to do is catch a native by himself and prove that we're friendly. Hide the robot, Clindar—somewhere in the woods where it can watch the village without being spotted. We've a week's practical anthropology ahead of us!'

It was three days before the biological tests showed that it would be safe to leave the ship. Even then Bertrond insisted on going alone—alone, that is, if one ignored the substantial company of the robot. With such an ally he was not afraid of this planet's larger beasts, and his body's natural defences could take care of the micro-organisms, so, at least, the analysers had assured him: and considering the complexity of the problem, they made remarkably few mistakes.

He stayed outside for an hour, enjoying himself cautiously, while his companions watched with envy. It would be another three days before they could be quite certain that it was safe to follow Bertrond's example. Meanwhile, they kept busy enough watching the village through the lenses of the robot, and recording everything they could with the cameras. They had moved the spaceship at night so that it was hidden in the depths of the forest, for they did not wish to be discovered until they were ready.

And all the while the news from home grew worse. Though their remoteness here at the edge of the universe deadened its impact, it lay heavily on their minds and sometimes overwhelmed them with a sense of futility. At any moment, they knew, the signal for recall might come as the Empire summoned up its last resources in its extremity. But until then they would continue their work as though pure knowledge were the only thing that mattered.

Seven days after landing, they were ready to make the experiment. They knew now what paths the villagers used when going hunting, and Bertrond chose one of the less frequented ways. Then he placed a chair firmly in the middle of the path and settled down to read a book.

It was not, of course, quite as simple as that: Bertrond had taken all imaginable precautions. Hidden in the undergrowth fifty yards away, the robot was watching through its telescopic lenses, and in its hand it held a small but deadly weapon. Controlling it from the spaceship, his fingers poised over the keyboard, Clindar waited to do what might be necessary.

24

That was the negative side of the plan: the positive side was more obvious. Lying at Bertrond's feet was the carcass of a small, horned animal which he hoped would be an acceptable gift to any hunter passing this way.

Two hours later the radio in his suit harness whispered a warning. Quite calmly, though the blood was pounding in his veins, Bertrond laid aside his book and looked down the trail. The savage was walking forward confidently enough, swinging a spear in his right hand. He paused for a moment when he saw Bertrond, then advanced more cautiously. He could tell that there was nothing to fear, for the stranger was slightly built and obviously unarmed.

When only twenty feet separated them, Bertrond gave a reassuring smile and rose slowly to his feet. He bent down, picked up the carcass, and carried it forward as an offering. The gesture would have been understood by any creature on any world, and it was understood here. The savage reached forward, took the animal, and threw it effortlessly over his shoulder. For an instant he stared into Bertrond's eyes with a fathomless expression; then he turned and walked back towards the village. Three times he glanced round to see if Bertrond was following, and each time Bertrond smiled and waved reassurance. The whole episode lasted little more than a minute. As the first contact between two races it was completely without drama, though not without dignity.

Bertrond did not move until the other had vanished from sight. Then he relaxed and spoke into his suit microphone.

'That was a pretty good beginning,' he said jubilantly. 'He wasn't in the least frightened, or even suspicious. I think he'll be back.'

'It still seems too good to be true,' said Altman's voice in his ear. 'I should have thought he'd have been either scared or hostile. Would *you* have accepted a lavish gift from a peculiar stranger with such little fuss?'

Bertrond was slowly walking back to the ship. The robot had now come out of cover and was keeping guard a few paces behind him.

'*I* wouldn't,' he replied, 'but I belong to a civilized community. Complete savages may react to strangers in many different ways, according to their past experience. Suppose this tribe has never had any enemies. That's quite possible on a large but sparsely populated planet. Then we may expect curiosity, but no fear at all.'

'If these people have no enemies,' put in Clindar, no longer fully occupied in controlling the robot, 'why have they got a stockade round the village?'

'I mean no *human* enemies,' replied Bertrond. 'If that's true, it simplifies our task immensely.'

'Do you think he'll come back?'

'Of course. If he's human as I think, curiosity and greed will make him return. In a couple of days we'll be bosom friends.'

Looked at dispassionately, it became a fantastic routine. Every morning the robot would go hunting under Clindar's direction, until it was now the deadliest killer in the jungle. Then Bertrond would wait until Yaan—which was the nearest they could get to his name—came striding confidently along the path. He came at the same time every day, and he always came alone. They wondered about this: did he wish to keep his great discovery to himself and thus get all the credit for his hunting prowess? If so, it showed unexpected foresight and cunning.

At first Yaan had departed at once with his prize, as if afraid that the donor of such a generous gift might change his mind. Soon, however, as Bertrond had hoped, he could be induced to stay for a while by simple conjuring tricks and a display of brightly coloured fabrics and crystals, in which he took a childlike delight. At last Bertrond was able to engage him in lengthy conversations, all of which were recorded as well as being filmed through the eyes of the hidden robot.

One day the philologists might be able to analyse this material; the best that Bertrond could do was to discover the meanings of a few simple verbs and nouns. This was made more difficult by the fact that Yaan not only used different words for the same thing, but sometimes the same word for different things.

Between these daily interviews, the ship travelled far, surveying the planet from the air and sometimes landing for more detailed examinations. Although several other human settlements were observed, Bertrond made no attempt to get in touch with them, for it was easy to see that they were all at much the same cultural level as Yaan's people.

It was, Bertrond often thought, a particularly bad joke on the part of fate that one of the galaxy's very few truly human races should have been discovered at this moment of time. Not long ago this would have been an event of supreme importance; now civilization was too hard-pressed to concern itself with these savage cousins waiting at the dawn of history.

Not until Bertrond was sure he had become part of Yaan's everyday life did he introduce him to the robot. He was showing Yaan the patterns in a kaleidoscope when Clindar brought the machine striding through the grass with its latest victim dangling across one metal arm. For the first time Yaan showed something akin to fear; but he relaxed at Bertrond's soothing words, though he continued to watch the advancing monster. It halted some distance away, and Bertrond walked forward to meet it. As he did so, the robot raised its arms and handed him the dead beast. He took it solemnly and carried it back to Yaan, staggering a little under the unaccustomed load.

Bertrond would have given a great deal to know just what Yaan was thinking as he accepted the gift. Was he trying to decide whether the robot was master or slave? Perhaps such conceptions as this were beyond his grasp: to him the robot might be merely another man, a hunter who was a friend of Bertrond.

Clindar's voice, slightly larger than life, came from the robot's speaker.

'It's astonishing how calmly he accepts us. Won't anything scare him?'

'You will keep judging him by your own standards,' replied Bertrond. 'Remember, his psychology is completely different, and much simpler. Now that he has confidence in me anything that I accept won't worry him.'

'I wonder if that will be true of all his race?' queried Altman. 'It's hardly safe to judge by a single specimen. I want to see what happens when we send the robot in to the village.'

'Hello!' exclaimed Bertrond. '*That* surprised him. He's never met a person who could speak with two voices before.'

'Do you think he'll guess the truth when he meets us?' said Clindar.

'No. The robot will be pure magic to him—but it won't be any more wonderful than fire and lightning and all the other forces he must already take for granted.'

'Well, what's the next move?' asked Altman, a little impatiently. 'Are you going to bring him to the ship, or will you go into the village first?'

Bertrond hesitated. 'I'm anxious not to do too much too quickly. You know the accidents that have happened with strange races when that's been tried. I'll let him think this over and when we get back tomorrow I'll try to persuade him to take the robot back to the village.'

In the hidden ship, Clindar reactivated the robot and started it moving again. Like Altman, he was growing a little impatient of this excessive caution, but on all matters relating to alien life-forms Bertrond was the expert, and they had to obey his orders.

There were times now when he almost wished he were a robot himself, devoid of feelings or emotions, able to watch the fall of a leaf or the death agonies of a world with equal detachment.

The sun was low when Yaan heard the great voice crying from the jungle. He recognized it at once, despite its inhuman volume: it was the voice of his friend calling him.

In the echoing silence, the life of the village came to a stop.

Even the children ceased their play: the only sound was the thin cry of a baby frightened by the sudden silence.

All eyes were upon Yaan as he walked swiftly to his hut and grasped the spear that lay beside the entrance. The stockade would soon be closed against the prowlers of the night, but he did not hesitate as he stepped out into the lengthening shadows. He was passing through the gates when once again that mighty voice summoned him, and now it held a note of urgency that came clearly across all the barriers of language and culture.

The shining giant who spoke with many voices met him a little way from the village and beckoned him to follow. There was no sign of Bertrond. They walked for almost a mile before they saw him in the distance, standing not far from the river's edge and staring out across the dark, slowly moving waters.

He turned as Yaan approached, yet for a moment seemed unaware of his presence. Then he gave a gesture of dismissal to the shining one, who withdrew into the distance.

Yaan waited. He was patient and, though he could never have expressed it in words, contented. When he was with Bertrond he felt the first intimations of that selfless, utterly irrational devotion his race would not fully achieve for many ages.

It was a strange tableau. Here at the river's brink two men were standing. One was dressed in a closely fitting uniform equipped with tiny, intricate mechanisms. The other was wearing the skin of an animal and was carrying a flint-tipped spear. Ten thousand generations lay between them, ten thousand generations and an immeasurable gulf of space. Yet they were both human. As she must often do in eternity, nature had repeated one of her basic patterns.

Presently Bertrond began to speak, walking to and fro in short, quick steps as he did so, and in his voice there was a trace of sadness.

'It's all over, Yaan. I'd hoped that with our knowledge we could have brought you out of barbarism in a dozen generations but now you will have to fight your way up from the jungle alone and it may take you a million years to do so. I'm sorry—there's so much we could have done. Even now I wanted to stay here, but Altman and Clindar talk of duty, and I suppose that they are right. There is little enough that we can do, but our world is calling and we must not forsake it.

'I wish you could understand me, Yaan. I wish you knew what I was saying. I'm leaving you these tools: some of them you will discover how to use, though as likely as not in a generation they'll be lost or forgotten. See how this blade cuts: it will be ages before your world can make its like. And guard this well: when you press the button—look! If you use it sparingly, it will give you light for years, though sooner or later it will die. As for these other things—find what use for them you can.

'Here come the first stars, up there in the east. Do you ever look at the stars, Yaan? I wonder how long it will be before you have discovered what they are, and I wonder what will have happened to us by then. Those stars are our homes, Yaan, and we cannot save them. Many have died already, in explosions so vast that I can imagine them no more than you. In a hundred thousand of your years, the light of those funeral pyres will reach your world and set its peoples wondering. By then, perhaps, your race will be reaching for the stars. I wish I could warn you against the mistakes we made, and which now will cost us all that we have won.

'It is well for your people, Yaan, that your world is here at the frontier of the universe. You may escape the doom that waits for us. One day, perhaps, your ships will go searching among the stars as we have done, and they may come upon the ruins of our worlds and wonder who we were. But they will never know that we met here by this river when your race was young.

'Here come my friends; they would give me no more time. Goodbye, Yaan—use well the things I have left you. They are your world's greatest treasures.'

Something huge, something that glittered in the starlight, was sliding down from the sky. It did not reach the ground, but came to rest a little way above the surface, and in utter silence a rectangle of light opened in its side. The shining giant appeared out of the night and stepped through the golden door. Bertrond followed, pausing for a moment at the threshold to wave back at Yaan. Then the darkness closed behind him.

No more swiftly than smoke drifts upward from a fire, the ship lifted away. When it was so small that Yaan felt he could hold it in his hands, it seemed to blur into a long line of light slanting upward into the stars. From the empty sky a peal of thunder echoed over the sleeping land: and Yaan knew at last that the gods were gone and would never come again.

For a long time he stood by the gently moving waters, and into his soul there came a sense of loss he was never to forget and never to understand. Then, carefully and reverently, he collected together the gifts that Bertrond had left.

Under the stars, the lonely figure walked homeward across a nameless land. Behind him the river flowed softly to the sea, winding through the fertile plains on which, more than a thousand centuries ahead, Yaan's descendants would build the great city they were to call Babylon.

Lenny

Isaac Asimov

United States Robots and Mechanical Men, Inc., had a problem. The problem was people.

Peter Bogert, Senior Mathematician, was on his way to Assembly when he encountered Alfred Lanning, Research Director. Lanning was bending his ferocious white eyebrows together and staring down across the railings into the computer room.

On the floor below the balcony, a trickle of humanity of both sexes and various ages was looking about curiously, while a guide intoned a set speech about robotic computing.

'This computer you see before you,' he said, 'is the largest of its type in the world. It contains five million three hundred thousand cryotrons and is capable of dealing simultaneously with over one hundred thousand variables. With its help, US Robots is able to design with precision the positronic brains of new models.

'The requirements are fed in on tape which is perforated by the action of this keyboard—something like a very complicated typewriter or linotype machine, except that it does not deal with letters but with concepts. Statements are broken down into the symbolic logic equivalents and those in turn converted to perforation patterns.

'The computer can, in less than one hour, present our scientists with a design for a brain which will give all the necessary positronic paths to make a robot . . . .'

Alfred Lanning looked up at last and noticed the other. 'Ah, Peter,' he said.

Bogert raised both hands to smooth down his already perfectly smooth and glossy head of black hair. He said, 'You don't look as though you think much of this, Alfred.'

Lanning grunted. The idea of public guided tours of US Robots was of fairly recent origin, and was supposed to serve a dual function. On the one hand, the theory went, it allowed people to see robots at close quarters and counter their almost instinctive fear of the mechanical objects through increased familiarity. And on the other hand, it was supposed to interest at least an occasional person in taking up robotics research as a life work.

'You know I don't,' Lanning said finally. 'Once a week, work is disrupted. Considering the man-hours lost, the return is insufficient.'

'Still no rise in job applications, then?'

'Oh, some, but only in the categories where the need isn't vital. It's research men that are needed. You know that. The trouble is that with robots forbidden on Earth itself, there's something unpopular about being a roboticist.'

'The damned Frankenstein complex,' said Bogert, consciously imitating one of the other's pet phrases.

Lanning missed the gentle jab. He said, 'I ought to be used to it, but I never will. You'd think that by now every human being on Earth would know that the Three Laws represented a perfect safeguard; that robots are simply not dangerous. Take this bunch.' He glowered down. 'Look at them. Most of them go through the robot assembly room for the thrill of fear, like riding a roller coaster. Then when they enter the room with the MEC model—damn it, Peter, a MEC model that will do nothing on God's green Earth but take two steps forward, say "Pleased to meet you, sir," shake hands, then take two steps back—they back away and mothers snatch up their kids. How do we expect to get brainwork out of such idiots?'

Bogert had no answer. Together, they stared down once again at the line of sightseers, now passing out of the computer room and into the positronic brain assembly section. Then they left. They did not, as it turned out, observe Mortimer W.

Jacobson, age sixteen—who, to do him complete justice, meant no harm whatever.

In fact, it could not even be said to be Mortimer's fault. The day of the week on which the tour took place was known to all workers. All devices in its path ought to have been carefully neutralized or locked, since it was unreasonable to expect human beings to withstand the temptation to handle knobs, keys, handles and pushbuttons. In addition, the guide ought to have been very carefully on the watch for those who succumbed.

But, at the time, the guide had passed into the next room and Mortimer was tailing the line. He passed the keyboard on which instructions were fed into the computer. He had no way of suspecting that the plans for a new robot design were being fed into it at the moment, or, being a good kid, he would have avoided the keyboard. He had no way of knowing that, by what amounted to almost criminal negligence, a technician had not inactivated the keyboard.

So Mortimer touched the keys at random as though he were playing a musical instrument.

He did not notice that a section of perforated tape stretched itself out of the instrument in another part of the room— soundlessly, unobtrusively.

Nor did the technician, when he returned, discover any signs of tampering. He felt a little uneasy at noticing that the keyboard was live, but did not think to check. After a few minutes, even his first trifling uneasiness was gone, and he continued feeding data into the computer.

As for Mortimer, neither then, nor ever afterwards, did he know what he had done.

The new LNE model was designed for the mining of boron in the asteroid belt. The boron hydrides were increasing in value yearly as primers for the proton micropiles that carried the ultimate load of power production on spaceships, and Earth's own meagre supply was running thin.

Physically, that meant that the LNE robots would have to be equipped with eyes sensitive to those lines prominent in the spectroscopic analysis of boron ores and the type of limbs most useful for the working up of ore to finished product. As always, though, the mental equipment was the major problem.

The first LNE positronic brain had been completed now. It was the prototype and would join all other prototypes in US Robots' collection. When finally tested, others would then be manufactured for leasing (never selling) to mining corporations.

LNE-prototype was complete now. Tall, straight, polished, it looked from outside like any of a number of not-too-specialized robot models.

The technician in charge, guided by the directions for testing in the *Handbook of Robotics*, said, 'How are you?'

The indicated answer was to have been, 'I am well and ready to begin my functions. I trust you are well, too,' or some trivial modification thereof.

This first exchange served no purpose but to show that the robot could hear, understand a routine question, and make a routine reply congruent with what one would expect of a robotic attitude. Beginning from there, one could pass on to more complicated matters that would test the different Laws and their interaction with the specialized knowledge of each particular model.

So the technician said, 'How are you?' He was instantly jolted by the nature of LNE-prototype's voice. It had a quality like no robotic voice he had ever heard (and he had heard many). It formed syllables like the chimes of a low-pitched celeste.

So surprising was this that it was only after several moments that the technician heard, in retrospect, the syllables that had been formed by those heavenly tones.

They were, 'Da, da, da, goo.'

35

The robot still stood tall and straight but its right hand crept upward and a finger went into its mouth.

The technician stared in absolute horror and bolted. He locked the door behind him and, from another room, put in an emergency call to Dr Susan Calvin.

Dr Susan Calvin was US Robots' (and, virtually, mankind's) only robopsychologist. She did not have to go very far in her testing of LNE-prototype before she called very peremptorily for a transcript of the computer-drawn plans of the positronic brain-paths and the taped instructions that had directed them. After some study, she, in turn, sent for Bogert.

Her iron-gray hair was drawn severely back; her cold face, with its strong vertical lines marked off by the horizontal gash of the pale, thin-lipped mouth, turned intensely upon him.

'What *is* this, Peter?'

Bogert studied the passages she pointed out with increasing stupefaction and said, 'Good Lord, Susan, it makes no sense.'

'It most certainly doesn't. How did it get into the instructions?'

The technician in charge, called upon, swore in all sincerity that it was none of his doing, and that he could not account for it. The computer checked out negative for all attempts at flaw-finding.

'The positronic brain,' said Susan Calvin thoughtfully, 'is past redemption. So many of the higher functions have been cancelled out by these meaningless directions that the result is very like a human baby.'

Bogert looked surprised, and Susan Calvin took on a frozen attitude at once, as she always did at the least expressed or implied doubt of her word. She said, 'We make every effort to make a robot as mentally like a man as possible. Eliminate what we call the adult functions and what is naturally left is a human infant, mentally speaking. Why do you look so surprised, Peter?'

LNE-prototype, who showed no signs of understanding

any of the things that were going on around it, suddenly slipped into a sitting position and began a minute examination of its feet.

Bogert stared at it. 'It's a shame to have to dismantle the creature. It's a handsome job.'

'Dismantle it?' said the robopsychologist forcefully.

'Of course, Susan. What's the use of this thing? Good Lord, if there's one object completely and abysmally useless it's a robot without a job it can perform. You don't pretend there's a job this thing can do, do you?'

'No, of course not.'

'Well, then?'

Susan Calvin said, stubbornly, 'I want to conduct more tests.'

Bogert looked at her with a moment's impatience, then shrugged. If there was one person at US Robots with whom it was useless to dispute, surely that was Susan Calvin. Robots were all she loved, and long association with them, it seemed to Bogert, had deprived her of any appearance of humanity. She was no more to be argued out of a decision than was a triggered micropile to be argued out of operating.

'What's the use?' he breathed; then aloud, hastily: 'Will you let us know when your tests are complete?'

'I will,' she said. 'Come, Lenny.'

(LNE, thought Bogert. That becomes Lenny. Inevitable.)

Susan Calvin held out her hand but the robot only stared at it. Gently, the robopsychologist reached for the robot's hand and took it. Lenny rose smoothly to its feet (its mechanical coordination, at least, worked well). Together they walked out, robot topping woman by two feet. Many eyes followed them curiously down the long corridors.

One wall of Susan Calvin's laboratory, the one opening directly off her private office, was covered with a highly magnified reproduction of a positronic-path chart. Susan Calvin had studied it with absorption for the better part of a month.

She was considering it now, carefully, tracing the blunted paths through their contortions. Behind her, Lenny sat on the floor, moving its legs apart and together, crooning meaningless syllables to itself in a voice so beautiful that one could listen to the nonsense and be ravished.

Susan Calvin turned to the robot, 'Lenny – Lenny—'

She repeated this patiently until finally Lenny looked up and made an inquiring sound. The robopsychologist allowed a glimmer of pleasure to cross her face fleetingly. The robot's attention was being gained in progressively shorter intervals.

She said, 'Raise your hand, Lenny. Hand – up. Hand – up.'

She raised her own hand as she said it, over and over.

Lenny followed the movement with its eyes. Up, down, up, down. Then it made an abortive gesture with its own hand and chimed, 'Eh – uh.'

'Very good, Lenny,' said Susan Calvin gravely. 'Try it again. Hand – up.'

Very gently, she reached out her own hand, took the robot's and raised it, lowered it. 'Hand – up. Hand – up.'

A voice from her office called and interrupted. 'Susan?'

Calvin halted with a tightening of her lips. 'What is it, Alfred?'

The research director walked in, and looked at the chart on the wall and at the robot. 'Still at it?'

'I'm at my work, yes.'

'Well, you know, Susan . . . .' He took out a cigar, staring at it hard, and made as though to bite off the end. In doing so, his eyes met the woman's stern look of disapproval; and he put the cigar away and began over. 'Well, you know, Susan, the LNE model is in production now.'

'So I've heard. Is there something in connection with it you wish of me?'

'No-o. Still, the mere fact that it is in production and is doing well means that working with this messed-up specimen is useless. Shouldn't it be scrapped?'

'In short, Alfred, you are annoyed that I am wasting my

so-valuable time. Feel relieved. My time is not being wasted. I am *working* with this robot.'

'But the work has no meaning.'

'I'll be the judge of that, Alfred.' Her voice was ominously quiet, and Lanning thought it wiser to shift his ground.

'Will you tell me what meaning it has? What are you doing with it right now, for instance?'

'I'm trying to get it to raise its hand on the word of command. I'm trying to get it to imitate the sound of the word.'

As though on cue, Lenny said, 'Eh-uh' and raised its hand waveringly.

Lanning shook his head. 'That voice is amazing. How does it happen?'

Susan Calvin said, 'I don't quite know. Its transmitter is a normal one. It could speak normally, I'm sure. It doesn't, however; it speaks like this as a consequence of something in the positronic paths that I have not yet pinpointed.'

'Well, pinpoint it, for heaven's sake. Speech like that might be useful.'

'Oh, then there is some possible use in my studies on Lenny?'

Lanning shrugged in embarrassment. 'Oh, well, it's a minor point.'

'I'm sorry you don't see the major points, then,' said Susan Calvin with asperity, 'which are much more important, but that's not my fault. Would you leave now, Alfred, and let me go on with my work?'

Lanning got to his cigar, eventually, in Bogert's office. He said, sourly, 'That woman is growing more peculiar daily.'

Bogert understood perfectly. In the US Robots and Mechanical Men, Inc., there was only one 'that woman'. He said, 'Is she still scuffing about with that pseudorobot— that Lenny of hers?'

'Trying to get it to talk, so help me.'

Bogert shrugged. 'Points up the company problem. I mean

about getting qualified personnel for research. If we had other robopsychologists, we could retire Susan. Incidentally, I presume the directors' meeting scheduled for tomorrow is for the purpose of dealing with the procurement problem?'

Lanning nodded and looked at his cigar as though it didn't taste good. 'Yes. Quality, though, not quantity. We've raised wages until there's a steady stream of applicants—those who are interested primarily in money. The trick is to get those who are interested primarily in robotics—a few more like Susan Calvin.'

'Hell, no. Not like her.'

'Well, not like her personally. But you'll have to admit, Peter, that she's single-minded about robots. She has no other interest in life.'

'I know. And that's exactly what makes her so unbearable.'

Lanning nodded. He had lost count of the many times it would have done his soul good to have fired Susan Calvin. He had also lost count of the number of millions of dollars she had at one time or another saved the company. She was a truly indispensable woman and would remain one until she died—or until they could lick the problem of finding men and women of her own high calibre who were interested in robotics research.

He said, 'I think we'll cut down on the tour business.'

Peter shrugged. 'If you say so. But meanwhile, seriously, what do we do about Susan? She can easily tie herself up with Lenny indefinitely. You know how she is when she gets what she considers an interesting problem.'

'What *can* we do?' said Lanning. 'If we become too anxious to pull her off, she'll stay on out of feminine contrariness. In the last analysis, we can't force her to do anything.'

The dark-haired mathematician smiled. 'I wouldn't ever apply the adjective "feminine" to any part of her.'

'Oh, well,' said Lanning grumpily. 'At least, it won't do anyone any actual harm.'

In that, if in nothing else, he was wrong.

The emergency signal is always a tension-making thing in any large industrial establishment. Such signals had sounded in the history of US Robots a dozen times—for fire, flood, riot and insurrection.

But one thing had never occurred in all that time. Never had the particular signal indicating 'Robot out of control' sounded. No one ever expected it to sound. It was only installed at government insistence. ('Damn the Frankenstein complex,' Lanning would mutter on those rare occasions when he thought of it.)

Now, finally, the shrill siren rose and fell at ten-second intervals, and practically no worker from the President of the Board of Directors down to the newest janitor's assistant recognized the significance of the strange sound for a few moments. After those moments passed, there was a massive convergence of armed guards and medical men to the indicated area of danger and US Robots was struck with paralysis.

Charles Randow, computing technician, was taken off to hospital level with a broken arm. There was no other damage. No other physical damage.

'But the moral damage,' roared Lanning, 'is beyond estimation.'

Susan Calvin faced him, murderously calm. 'You will do nothing to Lenny. Nothing. Do you understand?'

'Do *you* understand, Susan? That thing has hurt a human being. It has broken First Law. Don't you know what First Law is?'

'You will do nothing to Lenny.'

'For God's sake, Susan, do I have to tell *you* First Law? *A robot may not harm a human being or, through inaction, allow a human being to come to harm.* Our entire position depends on the fact that First Law is rigidly observed by all robots of all types. If the public should hear, and they will hear, that there was an exception, even one exception, we might be forced to close down altogether. Our only chance of survival would be to announce at once that the robot involved had been destroyed, explain the circumstances, and hope

41

that the public can be convinced that it will never happen again.'

'I would like to find out exactly what happened,' said Susan Calvin. 'I was not present at the time and I would like to know exactly what the Randow boy was doing in my laboratories without my permission.'

'The important thing that happened,' said Lanning, 'is obvious. Your robot struck Randow and the damn fool flashed the "Robot out of control" button and made a case of it. But your robot struck him and inflicted damage to the extent of a broken arm. The truth is your Lenny is so distorted it lacks First Law and it must be destroyed.'

'It does *not* lack First Law. I have studied its brain paths and know it does not lack it.'

'Then how could it strike a man?' Desperation turned him to sarcasm. 'Ask Lenny. Surely you have taught it to speak by now.'

Susan Calvin's cheeks flushed a painful pink. She said, 'I prefer to interview the victim. And in my absence, Alfred, I want my offices sealed tight, with Lenny inside. I want no one to approach him. If any harm comes to him while I am gone, this company will not see me again under any circumstances.'

'Will you agree to its destruction, if it has broken First Law?'

'Yes,' said Susan Calvin, 'because I know it hasn't.'

Charles Randow lay in bed with his arm set and in a cast. His major suffering was still from the shock of those few moments in which he thought a robot was advancing on him with murder in its positronic mind. No other human had ever had such reason to fear direct robotic harm as he had had just then. He had had a unique experience.

Susan Calvin and Alfred Lanning stood beside his bed now; Peter Bogert, who had met them on the way, was with them. Doctors and nurses had been shooed out.

Susan Calvin said, 'Now—what happened?'

Randow was daunted. He muttered, 'The thing hit me in the arm. It was coming at me.'

Calvin said, 'Move farther back in the story. What were you doing in my laboratory without authorization?'

The young computer swallowed, and the Adam's apple in his thin neck bobbed noticeably. He was high-cheek-boned and abnormally pale. He said, 'We all knew about your robot. The word is you were trying to teach it to talk like a musical instrument. There were bets going as to whether it talked or not. Some said—uh—you could teach a gatepost to talk.'

'I suppose,' said Susan Calvin freezingly, 'that is meant as a compliment. What did that have to do with you?'

'I was supposed to go in there and settle matters—see if it would talk, you know. We swiped a key to your place and I waited till you were gone and went in. We had a lottery on who was to do it. I lost.'

'Then?'

'I tried to get it to talk and it hit me.'

'What do you mean, you tried to get it to talk? How did you try?'

'I—I asked it questions, but it wouldn't say anything, and I had to give the thing a fair shake, so I kind of—yelled at it, and—'

'And?'

There was a long pause. Under Susan Calvin's unwavering stare, Randow finally said, 'I tried to scare it into saying something.' He added defensively, 'I had to give the thing a fair shake.'

'How did you try to scare it?'

'I pretended to take a punch at it.'

'And it brushed your arm aside?'

'It *hit* my arm.'

'Very well. That's all.' To Lanning and Bogert, she said, 'Come, gentlemen.'

At the doorway, she turned back to Randow. 'I can settle

the bets going around, if you are still interested. Lenny can speak a few words quite well.'

They said nothing until they were in Susan Calvin's office. Its walls were lined with her books, some of which she had written herself. It retained the patina of her own frigid, carefully-ordered personality. It had only one chair in it and she sat down. Lanning and Bogert remained standing.

She said, 'Lenny only defended itself. That is the Third Law: *A robot must protect its own existence.*'

'*Except,*' said Lanning forcefully, '*when this conflicts with the First or Second Laws*. Complete the statement! Lenny had no right to defend itself in any way at the cost of harm, however minor, to a human being.'

'Nor did it,' shot back Calvin, '*knowingly*. Lenny has an aborted brain. It has no way of knowing its own strength or the weakness of humans. In brushing aside the threatening arm of a human being it could not know the bone would break. In human terms, no moral blame can be attached to an individual who honestly cannot differentiate good and evil.'

Bogert interrupted, soothingly, 'Now, Susan, *we* don't blame. *We* understand that Lenny is the equivalent of a baby, humanly speaking, and we don't blame it. But the public will. US Robots will be closed down.'

'Quite the opposite. If you had the brains of a flea, Peter, you would see that this is the opportunity US Robots is waiting for. That this will solve its problems.'

Lanning hunched his white eyebrows low. He said, softly, 'What problems, Susan?'

'Isn't the corporation concerned about maintaining our research personnel at the present—heaven help us—high level?'

'We certainly are.'

'Well, what are you offering prospective researchers? Excitement? Novelty? The thrill of piercing the unknown? No! You offer them salaries and the assurance of no problems.'

Bogert said, 'How do you mean, no problems?'

'Are there problems?' shot back Susan Calvin. 'What kind of robots do we turn out? Fully developed robots, fit for their tasks. And industry tells us what it needs; a computer designs the brain; machinery forms the robot; and there it is, complete and done. Peter, some time ago you asked me with reference to Lenny what its use was. What's the use, you said, of a robot that was not designed for any job? Now I ask you— what's the use of a robot designed for only one job? It begins and ends in the same place. The LNE models mine boron. If beryllium is needed, they are useless. If boron technology enters a new phase, they become useless. A human being so designed would be subhuman. A robot so designed is sub-robotic.'

'Do you want a versatile robot?' asked Lanning incredulously.

'Why not?' demanded the robopsychologist. 'Why not? I've been handed a robot with a brain almost completely stultified. I've been teaching it, and you, Alfred, asked me what was the use of that. Perhaps very little as far as Lenny itself is concerned since it will never progress beyond the five year old level on a human scale. But what's the use in general? A very great deal, if you consider it as a study in the abstract problem of *learning how to teach robots.* I have learned ways to short-circuit neighbouring pathways in order to create new ones. More study will yield better, more subtle and more efficient techniques of doing so.'

'Well?'

'Suppose you started with a positronic brain that had all the basic pathways carefully outlined but none of the secondaries. Suppose you then started creating secondaries. You could sell basic robots designed for instruction; robots that could be modelled to a job, and then modelled to another, if necessary. Robots would become as versatile as human beings. *Robots could learn!*'

They stared at her.

She said, impatiently, 'You still don't understand, do you?'

'I understand what you are saying,' said Lanning.

'Don't you understand that with a completely new field of research and completely new techniques to be developed, with a completely new area of the unknown to be penetrated, youngsters will feel a new urge to enter robotics? Try it and see.'

'May I point out,' said Bogert smoothly, 'that this is dangerous. Beginning with ignorant robots such as Lenny will mean that one could never trust First Law—exactly as turned out in Lenny's case.'

'Exactly. Advertise the fact.'

'*Advertise it!*'

'Of course. Broadcast the danger. Explain that you will set up a new research institute on the moon, if Earth's population chooses not to allow this sort of thing to go on upon Earth, but stress the danger to the possible applicants by all means.'

Lanning said, 'For God's sake, why?'

'Because the spice of danger will add to the lure. Do you think nuclear technology involves no danger and spationautics no peril? Has your lure of absolute security been doing the trick for you? Has it helped you to cater to the Frankenstein complex you all despise so? Try something else then, something that has worked in other fields.'

There was a sound from beyond the door that led to Calvin's personal laboratories. It was the chiming sound of Lenny.

The robopsychologist broke off instantly, listening. She said, 'Excuse me. I think Lenny is calling me.'

'Can it call you?' said Lanning.

'I said I've managed to teach it a few words.' She stepped toward the door, a little flustered. 'If you will wait for me—'

They watched her leave and were silent for a moment. Then Lanning said, 'Do you think there's anything to what she says, Peter?'

'Just possibly, Alfred,' said Bogert. 'Just possibly. Enough for us to bring the matter up at the directors' meeting and see what they say. After all, the fat *is* in the fire. A robot has harmed a human being and knowledge of it is public. As Susan says, we might as well try to turn the matter to our advantage. Of course, I distrust her motives in all this.'

'How do you mean?'

'Even if all she has said is perfectly true, it is only a rationalization as far as she is concerned. Her motive in all this is her desire to hold on to this robot. If we pressed her' (and the mathematician smiled at the incongruous literal meaning of the phrase), 'she would say it was to continue learning techniques of teaching robots, but I think she has found another use for Lenny. A rather unique one that would fit only Susan of all women.'

'I don't get your drift.'

Bogert said, 'Did you hear what the robot was calling?'

'Well, no, I didn't quite—' began Lanning, when the door opened suddenly, and both men stopped talking at once.

Susan Calvin stepped in again, looking about uncertainly. 'Have either of you seen—I'm positive I had it somewhere about—Oh, there it is.'

She ran to a corner of one bookcase and picked up an object of intricate metal webbery, dumb-bell shaped and hollow, with variously-shaped metal pieces inside each hollow, just too large to be able to fall out of the webbing.

As she picked it up, the metal pieces within moved and struck together, clicking pleasantly. It struck Lanning that the object was a kind of robotic version of a baby rattle.

As Susan Calvin opened the door again to pass through, Lenny's voice chimed again from within. This time, Lanning heard it clearly as it spoke the words Susan Calvin had taught it.

In heavenly celeste-like sounds, it called out, 'Mommie, I want you. I want you, Mommie.'

And the footsteps of Susan Calvin could be heard hurrying eagerly across the laboratory floor toward the only kind of baby she could ever have or love.

A Walk in the Dark

Arthur C. Clarke

Robert Armstrong had walked just over two miles, as far as he could judge, when his torch failed. He stood still for a moment, unable to believe that such a misfortune could really have befallen him. Then, half maddened with rage, he hurled the useless instrument away. It landed somewhere in the darkness, disturbing the silence of this little world. A metallic echo came ringing back from the low hills: then all was quiet again.

This, thought Armstrong, was the ultimate misfortune. Nothing more could happen to him now. He was even able to laugh bitterly at his luck, and resolved never again to imagine that the fickle goddess had ever favoured him. Who would have believed that the only tractor at Camp IV would have broken down when he was just setting off for Port Sanderson? He recalled the frenzied repair work, the relief when the second start had been made—and the final debacle when the caterpillar track had jammed.

It was no use then regretting the lateness of his departure: he could not have foreseen these accidents, and it was still a good four hours before the 'Canopus' took off. He *had* to catch her, whatever happened; no other ship would be touching at this world for another month.

Apart from the urgency of his business, four more weeks on this out of the way planet were unthinkable.

There had been only one thing to do. It was lucky that Port Sanderson was little more than six miles from the camp—not a great distance, even on foot. He had had to leave all his equipment behind but it could follow on the next ship and he could manage without it. The road was poor, merely stamped out of the rock by one of the Board's hundred-ton crushers, but there was no fear of going astray.

Even now, he was in no real danger, though he might well be too late to catch the ship. Progress would be slow, for he dare not risk losing the road in this region of canyons and enigmatic tunnels that had never been explored. It was, of course, pitch-dark. Here at the edge of the galaxy the stars were so few and scattered that their light was negligible. The strange crimson sun of this lonely world would not rise for many hours, and although five of the little moons were in the sky they could barely be seen by the unaided eye. Not one of them could even cast a shadow.

Armstrong was not the man to bewail his luck for long. He began to walk slowly along the road, feeling its texture with his feet. It was, he knew, fairly straight except where it wound through Carver's Pass. He wished he had a stick or something to probe the way before him, but he would have to rely for guidance on the feel of the ground.

It was terribly slow at first, until he gained confidence. He had never known how difficult it was to walk in a straight line. Although the feeble stars gave him his bearings, again and again he found himself stumbling among the virgin rocks at the edge of the crude roadway. He was travelling in long zigzags that took him to alternate sides of the road. Then he would stub his toes against the bare rock and grope his way back onto the hard-packed surface once again.

Presently it settled down to a routine. It was impossible to estimate his speed; he could only struggle along and hope for the best. There were four miles to go—four miles and as many hours. It should be easy enough, unless he lost his way. But he dared not think of that.

Once he had mastered the technique he could afford the luxury of thought. He could not pretend that he was enjoying the experience, but he had been in much worse positions before. As long as he remained on the road, he was perfectly safe. He had been hoping that as his eyes became adapted to the starlight he would be able to see the way, but he now knew that the whole journey would be blind. The discovery gave him a vivid sense of his remoteness from the heart of the galaxy. On a night as clear as this, the skies of almost any other planet would have been blazing with stars. Here at this outpost of the universe the sky held perhaps a hundred faintly gleaming points of light, as useless as the five ridiculous moons on which no one had ever bothered to land.

A slight change in the road interrupted his thoughts. Was there a curve here, or had he veered off to the right again? He moved very slowly along the invisible and ill-defined border. Yes, there was no mistake: the road was bending to the left. He tried to remember its appearance in the daytime, but he had only seen it once before. Did this mean that he was nearing the Pass? He hoped so, for the journey would then be half completed.

He peered ahead into the blackness, but the ragged line of the horizon told him nothing. Presently he found that the road had straightened itself again and his spirits sank. The entrance to the Pass must still be some way ahead: there were at least four miles to go.

Four miles—how ridiculous the distance seemed! How long would it take the 'Canopus' to travel four miles? He doubted if man would measure so short an interval of time. And how many trillions of miles had he, Robert Armstrong, travelled in his life? It must have reached a staggering total by now, for in the last twenty years he had scarcely stayed more than a month at a time on any single world. This very year, he had twice made the crossing of the galaxy, and that was a notable journey even in these days of the phantom drive.

He tripped over a loose stone, and the jolt brought him back to reality. It was no use, here, thinking of ships that could eat up the light-years. He was facing nature, with no weapons but his own strength and skill.

It was strange that it took him so long to identify the real cause of his uneasiness. The last four weeks had been very full, and the rush of his departure, coupled with the annoyance and anxiety caused by the tractor's breakdowns, had driven everything else from his mind. Moreover, he had always prided himself on his hardheadedness and lack of imagination. Until now, he had forgotten all about that first evening at the Base, when the crews had regaled him with the usual tall yarns concocted for the benefit of newcomers.

It was then that the old Base clerk had told the story of his walk by night from Port Sanderson to the camp, and of what had trailed him through Carver's Pass, keeping always beyond the limit of his torchlight. Armstrong, who had heard such tales on a score of worlds, had paid it little attention at the time. This planet, after all, was known to be uninhabited. But logic could not dispose of the matter as easily as that. Suppose, after all, there was some truth in the old man's fantastic tale . . . ?

It was not a pleasant thought, and Armstrong did not intend to brood upon it. But he knew that if he dismissed it out of hand it would continue to prey on his mind. The only way to conquer imaginary fears was to face them boldly; he would have to do that now.

His strongest argument was the complete barrenness of this world and its utter desolation, though against that one could set many counterarguments, as indeed the old clerk had done. Man had only lived on this planet for twenty years, and much of it was still unexplored. No one could deny that the tunnels out in the wasteland were rather puzzling, but everyone believed them to be volcanic vents. Though, of course, life often crept into such places. With a shudder he remembered the giant polyps that had snared the first explorers of Vargon III.

It was all very inconclusive. Suppose, for the sake of argument, one granted the existence of life here. What of that?

The vast majority of life forms in the universe were completely indifferent to man. Some, of course, like the gas-beings of Alcoran or the roving wave-lattices of Shandaloon, could not even detect him but passed through or around him as if he did not exist. Others were merely inquisitive, some embarrassingly friendly. There were few indeed that would attack unless provoked.

Nevertheless, it was a grim picture that the old stores clerk had painted. Back in the warm, well-lighted smoking-room, with the drinks going around, it had been easy enough to laugh at it. But here in the darkness, miles from any human settlement, it was very different.

It was almost a relief when he stumbled off the road again and had to grope with his hands until he found it once more. This seemed a very rough patch, and the road was scarcely distinguishable from the rocks around. In a few minutes, however, he was safely on his way again.

It was unpleasant to see how quickly his thoughts returned to the same disquieting subject. Clearly it was worrying him more than he cared to admit.

He drew consolation from one fact: it had been quite obvious that no one at the base had believed the old fellow's story. Their questions and banter had proved that. At the time, he had laughed as loudly as any of them. After all, what *was* the evidence? A dim shape, just seen in the darkness, that might well have been an oddly formed rock. And the curious clicking noise that had so impressed the old man—anyone could imagine such sounds at night if they were sufficiently overwrought. If it had been hostile, why hadn't the creature come any closer? 'Because it was afraid of my light,' the old chap had said. Well, that was plausible enough: it would explain why nothing had ever been seen in the daylight. Such a creature might live underground, only emerging at night—damn it, why was he taking the old idiot's ravings so seriously! Armstrong got control of his thoughts again. If he went on this way, he told himself angrily, he would soon be seeing and hearing a whole menagerie of monsters.

There was, of course, one factor that disposed of the ridiculous story at once. It was really very simple; he felt sorry he hadn't thought of it before. *What would such a creature live on?* There was not even a trace of vegetation on the whole of the planet. He laughed to think that the bogy could be disposed of so easily—and in the same instant felt annoyed with himself for not laughing aloud. If he was so sure of his reasoning, why not whistle, or sing, or do anything to keep up his spirits? He put the question fairly to himself as a test of his manhood. Half-ashamed, he had to admit that he was still afraid—afraid because 'there *might* be something in it, after all'. But at least his analysis had done him some good.

It would have been better if he had left it there, and remained half-convinced by his argument. But a part of his mind was still busily trying to break down his careful reasoning. It succeeded only too well, and when he remembered the plant-beings of Xantil Major the shock was so unpleasant that he stopped dead in his tracks.

Now the plant-beings of Xantil were not in any way horrible. They were in fact extremely beautiful creatures. But what made them appear so distressing now was the knowledge that they could live for indefinite periods with no food whatsoever. All the energy they needed for their strange lives they extracted from cosmic radiation—and that was almost as intense here as anywhere else in the universe.

He had scarcely thought of one example before others crowded into his mind and he remembered the life form on Trantor Beta, which was the only one known capable of directly utilizing atomic energy. That too had lived on an utterly barren world, very much like this....

Armstrong's mind was rapidly splitting into two distinct portions, each trying to convince the other and neither wholly succeeding. He did not realize how far his morale had gone until he found himself holding his breath lest it conceal any sound from the darkness about him. Angrily, he cleared his mind of the rubbish that had been gathering there and turned once more to the immediate problem.

There was no doubt that the road was slowly rising, and the silhouette of the horizon seemed much higher in the sky. The road began to twist, and suddenly he was aware of great rocks on either side of him. Soon only a narrow ribbon of sky was still visible, and the darkness became, if possible, even more intense.

Somehow, he felt safer with the rock walls surrounding him: it meant that he was protected except in two directions. Also, the road had been levelled more carefully and it was easy to keep to it. Best of all, he knew now that the journey was more than half completed.

For a moment his spirits began to rise. Then, with maddening perversity, his mind went back into the old grooves again. He remembered that it was on the far side of Carver's Pass that the old clerk's adventure had taken place—if it had ever happened at all.

In half a mile, he would be out in the open again, out of the protection of these sheltering rocks. The thought seemed doubly horrible now and he already felt a sense of nakedness. He could be attacked from any direction and he would be utterly helpless....

Until now, he had still retained some self-control. Very resolutely he had kept his mind away from the one fact that gave some colour to the old man's tale—the single piece of evidence that had stopped the banter in the crowded room back at the camp and brought a sudden hush upon the company. Now, as Armstrong's will weakened, he recalled again the words that had struck a momentary chill even in the warm comfort of the Base building.

The little clerk had been very insistent on one point. He had never heard any sound of pursuit from the dim shape sensed, rather than seen, at the limit of his light. There was no scuffling of claws or hoofs on rock, nor even the clatter of displaced stones. It was as if, so the old man had declared in that solemn manner of his, 'as if the thing that was following could see perfectly in the darkness, and had many small legs or pads so that it could move swiftly and easily over the rock—like a giant caterpillar or one of the carpet-things of Kralkor II.'

Yet, although there had been no noise of pursuit, there had

been one sound that the old man had caught several times. It was so unusual that its very strangeness made it doubly ominous. It was a faint but horribly persistent *clicking*.

The old fellow had been able to describe it very vividly — much too vividly for Armstrong's liking now.

'Have you ever listened to a large insect crunching its prey?' he said. 'Well, it was just like that. I imagine that a crab makes exactly the same noise with its claws when it clashes them together. It was a — what's the word? — a *chitinous* sound.'

At this point, Armstrong remembered laughing loudly. (Strange, how it was all coming back to him now.) But no one else had laughed, though they had been quick to do so earlier. Sensing the change of tone, he had sobered at once and asked the old man to continue his story. How he wished now that he had stifled his curiosity!

It had been quickly told. The next day, a party of sceptical technicians had gone into the no-man's-land beyond Carver's Pass. They were not sceptical enough to leave their guns behind, but they had no cause to use them for they found no trace of any living thing. There were the inevitable pits and tunnels, glistening holes down which the light of the torches rebounded endlessly until it was lost in the distance — but the planet was riddled with them.

Though the party found no sign of life, it discovered one thing it did not like at all. Out in the barren and unexplored land beyond the Pass they had come upon an even larger tunnel than the rest. Near the mouth of that tunnel was a massive rock, half embedded in the ground. And the sides of that rock had been worn away *as if it had been used as an enormous whetstone.*

No less than five of those present had seen this disturbing rock. None of them could explain it satisfactorily as a natural formation, but they still refused to accept the old man's story. Armstrong had asked them if they had ever put it to the test. There had been an uncomfortable silence. Then big Andrew Hargraves had said: 'Hell, who'd walk out to the

Pass at night just for fun!' and had left it at that. Indeed, there was no other record of anyone walking from Port Sanderson to the camp by night, or for that matter by day. During the hours of light, no unprotected human being could live in the open beneath the rays of the enormous, lurid sun that seemed to fill half the sky. And no one would walk six miles, wearing radiation armour, if the tractor was available.

Armstrong felt that he was leaving the Pass. The rocks on either side were falling away, and the road was no longer as firm and well packed as it had been. He was coming out into the open plain once more, and somewhere not far away in the darkness was that enigmatic pillar that might have been used for sharpening monstrous fangs or claws. It was not a reassuring thought, but he could not get it out of his mind.

Feeling distinctly worried now, Armstrong made a great effort to pull himself together. He would try to be rational again; he would think of business, the work he had done at the camp—anything but this infernal place. For a while, he succeeded quite well. But presently, with a maddening persistence, every train of thought came back to the same point. He could not get out of his mind the picture of that inexplicable rock and its appalling possibilities. Over and over again he found himself wondering how far away it was, whether he had already passed it, and whether it was on his right or his left....

The ground was quite flat again, and the road drove on straight as an arrow. There was one gleam of consolation: Port Sanderson could not be much more than two miles away. Armstrong had no idea how long he had been on the road. Unfortunately his watch was not illuminated and he could only guess at the passage of time. With any luck, the 'Canopus' should not take off for another two hours at least. But he could not be sure, and now another fear began to enter his mind—the dread that he might see a vast constellation of lights rising swiftly into the sky ahead, and know that all this agony of mind had been in vain.

He was not zigzagging so badly now, and seemed to be

able to anticipate the edge of the road before stumbling off it. It was probable, he cheered himself by thinking, that he was travelling almost as fast as if he had a light. If all went well, he might be nearing Port Sanderson in thirty minutes — a ridiculously small space of time. How he would laugh at his fears when he strolled into his already reserved state-room in the 'Canopus,' and felt that peculiar quiver as the phantom drive hurled the great ship far out of this system, back to the clustered star-clouds near the centre of the galaxy — back toward Earth itself, which he had not seen for so many years. One day, he told himself, he really must visit Earth again. All his life he had been making the promise, but always there had been the same answer — lack of time. Strange, wasn't it, that such a tiny planet should have played so enormous a part in the development of the universe, should even have come to dominate worlds far wiser and more intelligent than itself!

Armstrong's thoughts were harmless again, and he felt calmer. The knowledge that he was nearing Port Sanderson was immensely reassuring and he deliberately kept his mind on familiar, unimportant matters. Carver's Pass was already far behind, and with it that thing he no longer intended to recall. One day, if he ever returned to this world, he would visit the pass in the daytime and laugh at his fears. In twenty minutes now, they would have joined the nightmares of his childhood.

It was almost a shock, though one of the most pleasant shocks he had ever known, when he saw the lights of Port Sanderson come up over the horizon. The curvature of this little world was very deceptive: it did not seem right that a planet with a gravity almost as great as Earth's should have a horizon so close at hand. One day, someone would have to discover what lay at this world's core to give it so great a density. Perhaps the many tunnels would help — it was an unfortunate turn of thought, but the nearness of his goal had robbed it of terror now. Indeed, the thought that he might really be in danger seemed to give his adventure a certain piquancy and heightened interest. Nothing could happen to him now, with ten minutes to go and the lights of the Port already in sight.

A few minutes later, his feelings changed abruptly when he came to the sudden bend in the road. He had forgotten the chasm that caused his detour, and added half a mile to the journey. Well, what of it? he thought stubbornly. An extra half-mile would make no difference now—another ten minutes, at the most.

It was very disappointing when the lights of the city vanished. Armstrong had not remembered the hill which the road was skirting; perhaps it was only a low ridge, scarcely noticeable in the daytime. But by hiding the lights of the port it had taken away his chief talisman and left him again at the mercy of his fears.

Very unreasonably, his intelligence told him, he began to think how horrible it would be if anything happened now, so near the end of the journey. He kept the worst of his fears at bay for a while, hoping desperately that the lights of the city would soon reappear. But as the minutes dragged on, he realized that the ridge must be longer than he imagined. He tried to cheer himself by the thought that the city would be all the nearer when he saw it again, but somehow logic seemed to have failed him now. For presently he found himself doing something he had not stooped to, even out in the waste by Carver's Pass.

He stopped, turned slowly round, and with bated breath listened until his lungs were nearly bursting.

The silence was uncanny, considering how near he must be to the Port. There was certainly no sound from behind him. Of course, there wouldn't be, he told himself angrily. But he was immensely relieved. The thought of that faint and insistent clicking had been haunting him for the last hour.

So friendly and familiar was the noise that did reach him at last that the anticlimax almost made him laugh aloud. Drifting through the still air from a source clearly not more than a mile away came the sound of a landing-field tractor, perhaps one of the machines loading the 'Canopus' itself. In a matter of seconds, thought Armstrong, he would be around this ridge with the Port only a few hundred yards ahead. The journey was nearly ended. In a few moments, this evil plain would be no more than a fading nightmare.

It seemed terribly unfair: so little time, such a small fraction of a human life, was all he needed now. But the gods have always been unfair to man, and now they were enjoying their little jest. For there could be no mistaking the rattle of monstrous claws in the darkness *ahead of him*.

The Murderer

Ray Bradbury

Music moved with him in the white halls. He passed an office door: 'The Merry Widow Waltz'. Another door: 'Afternoon of a Faun'. A third: 'Kiss Me Again'. He turned into a cross corridor: 'The Sword Dance' buried him in cymbals, drums, pots, pans, knives, forks, thunder, and tin lightning. All washed away as he hurried through an anteroom where a secretary sat nicely stunned by Beethoven's Fifth. He moved himself before her eyes like a hand; she didn't see him.

His wrist radio buzzed.

'Yes?'

'This is Lee, Dad. Don't forget about my allowance.'

'Yes, son, yes. I'm busy.'

'Just didn't want you to forget, Dad,' said the wrist radio. Tchaikovsky's 'Romeo and Juliet' swarmed about the voice and flushed into the long halls.

The psychiatrist moved in the beehive of offices, in the crosspollination of themes, Stravinsky mating with Bach, Haydn unsuccessfully repulsing Rachmaninoff, Schubert slain by Duke Ellington. He nodded to the humming secretaries and the whistling doctors fresh to their morning work. At his office he checked a few papers with his stenographer, who sang under her breath, then phoned the police captain upstairs. A few minutes later a red light blinked, a voice said from the ceiling:

'Prisoner delivered to Interview Chamber Nine.'

He unlocked the chamber door, stepped in, heard the door lock behind him.

'Go away,' said the prisoner, smiling.

The psychiatrist was shocked by that smile. A very sunny, pleasant warm thing, a thing that shed bright light upon the room. Dawn among the dark hills. High noon at midnight, that smile. The blue eyes sparkled serenely above that display of self-assured dentistry.

'I'm here to help you,' said the psychiatrist, frowning. Something was wrong with the room. He had hesitated the moment he entered. He glanced around. The prisoner laughed. 'If you're wondering why it's so quiet in here, I just kicked the radio to death.'

Violent, thought the doctor.

The prisoner read this thought, smiled, put out a gentle hand. 'No, only to machines that yak-yak-yak.'

Bits of the wall radio's tubes and wires lay on the grey carpeting. Ignoring these, feeling that smile upon him like a heat lamp, the psychiatrist sat across from his patient in the unusual silence which was like the gathering of a storm.

'You're Mr Albert Brock, who calls himself The Murderer?'

Brock nodded pleasantly. 'Before we start . . .' He moved quietly and quickly to detach the wrist radio from the doctor's arm. He tucked it in his teeth like a walnut, gritted and heard it crack, handed it back to the appalled psychiatrist as if he had done them both a favour. 'That's better.'

The psychiatrist stared at the ruined machine. 'You're running up quite a damage bill.'

'I don't care,' smiled the patient. 'As the old song goes: "Don't Care What Happens to Me!"' He hummed it.

The psychiatrist said: 'Shall we start?'

'Fine. The first victim, or one of the first, was my telephone. Murder most foul. I shoved it in the kitchen Insinkerator! Stopped the disposal unit in midswallow. Poor thing strangled to death. After that I shot the television set!'

The psychiatrist said, 'Mmm.'

'Fired six shots right through the cathode. Made a beautiful tinkling crash, like a dropped chandelier.'

'Nice imagery.'

'Thanks, I always dreamt of being a writer.'

'Suppose you tell me when you first began to hate the telephone.'

'It frightened me as a child. Uncle of mine called it the Ghost Machine. Voices without bodies. Scared the living hell out of me. Later in life I was never comfortable. Seemed to me a phone was an impersonal instrument. If it *felt* like it, it let your personality go through its wires. If it didn't *want* to, it just drained your personality away until what slipped through at the other end was some cold fish of a voice all steel, copper, plastic, no warmth, no reality. It's easy to say the wrong thing on telephones; the telephone changes your meaning on you. First thing you know, you've made an enemy. Then, of course, the telephone's such a *convenient* thing; it just sits there and *demands* you call someone who doesn't want to be called. Friends were always calling, calling, calling me. Hell, I hadn't any time of my own. When it wasn't the telephone it was the television, the radio, the phonograph. When it wasn't the televison or radio or the phonograph it was motion pictures at the corner theatre, motion pictures projected, with commercials on low-lying cumulus clouds. It doesn't rain rain any more, it rains soap-suds. When it wasn't High-Fly Cloud advertisements, it was music by Mozzek in every restaurant; music and commercials on the buses I rode to work. When it wasn't music, it was interoffice communications, and my horror chamber of a radio wristwatch on which my friends and my wife phoned every five minutes. What is there about such "conveniences" that makes them so *temptingly* convenient? The average man thinks, Here I am, time on my hands, and there on my wrist is a wrist telephone, so why not just buzz old Joe up, eh? "Hello, hello!" I love my friends, my wife, humanity, very much, but when one minute my wife calls to say, "Where are you *now*, dear?" and a friend calls and says, "Got the best off-colour joke to tell you. Seems there was a guy —— " And a stranger calls and cries out, "This is the Find-Fax Poll. What gum are you chewing at this very *instant!*" Well!'

'How did you feel during the week?'

'The fuse lit. On the edge of the cliff. That same afternoon I did what I did at the office.'

'Which was?'

'I poured a paper cup of water into the intercommunications system.'

The psychiatrist wrote on his pad.

'And the system shorted?'

'Beautifully! The Fourth of July on wheels! My God, stenographers ran around looking *lost*! What an uproar!'

'Felt better temporarily, eh?'

'Fine! Then I got the idea at noon of stomping my wrist radio on the sidewalk. A shrill voice was just yelling out of it at me, "This is People's Poll Number Nine. What did you eat for lunch?" when I kicked the Jesus out of the wrist radio!'

'Felt even *better*, eh?'

'It *grew* on me!' Brock rubbed his hands together. 'Why didn't I start a solitary revolution, deliver man from certain "conveniences"? "Convenient for who?" I cried. Convenient for friends: "Hey, Al, thought I'd call you from the locker room out here at Green Hills. Just made a sockdolager hole in one! A hole in one, Al! A *beautiful* day. Having a shot of whiskey now. Thought you'd want to know, Al!" Convenient for my office, so when I'm in the field with my radio car there's no moment when I'm not in touch. In *touch! There's* a slimy phrase. Touch, hell. *Gripped!* Pawed, rather. Mauled and massaged and pounded by FM voices. You can't leave your car without checking in: "Have stopped to visit gas-station men's room." "Okay, Brock, step on it!" "Brock, What *took* you so long?" "Sorry, sir," "Watch it next time, Brock." "*Yes, sir!*" So, do you know what I did, Doctor? I bought a quart of French chocolate icecream and spooned it into the car radio transmitter.'

'Was there any *special* reason for selecting French chocolate icecream to spoon into the broadcasting unit?'

Brock thought about it and smiled. 'It's my favourite flavour.'

'Oh,' said the doctor.

'I figured, hell, what's good enough for me is good enough for the radio transmitter.'

'What made you think of spooning *icecream* into the radio?'

'It was a hot day.'

The doctor paused.

'And what happened next?'

'Silence happened next. God, it was *beautiful.* That car radio cackling all day, Brock go here, Brock go there, Brock check in, Brock check out, okay Brock, hour lunch, Brock, lunch over, Brock, Brock, Brock. Well, that silence was like putting icecream in my ears.'

'You seem to like icecream a lot.'

'I just rode around feeling of the silence. It's a big bolt of the nicest, softest flannel ever made. Silence. A whole hour of it. I just sat in my car; smiling, feeling of that flannel with my ears. I felt *drunk* with Freedom!'

'Go on.'

'Then I got the idea of the portable diathermy machine. I rented one, took it on the bus going home that night. There sat all the tired commuters with their wrist radios, talking to their wives, saying, "Now I'm at Forty-third, now I'm at Forty-fourth, here I am at Forty-ninth, now turning at Sixty-first." One husband cursing, "Well, get *out* of that bar, damn it, and get home and get dinner started, I'm at Seventieth!" And the transit-system radio playing "Tales from the Vienna Woods", a canary singing words about a first-rate wheat cereal. Then—I switched on my diathermy! Static! Interference! All wives cut off from husbands grousing about a hard day at the office. All husbands cut off from wives who had just seen their children break a window! The "Vienna Woods" chopped down, the canary mangled! *Silence!* A terrible, unexpected silence. The bus inhabitants faced with having to converse with each other. Panic! Sheer, animal panic!'

'The police seized you?'

'The bus *had* to stop. After all, the music *was* being scrambled, husbands and wives *were* out of touch with reality. Pandemonium, riot, and chaos. Squirrels chattering in cages! A trouble unit arrived, triangulated on me instantly, had me reprimanded, fined, and home, minus my diathermy machine, in jig time.'

'Mr Brock, may I suggest that so far your whole pattern here is not very—practical? If you didn't like transit radios or office radios or car business radios, why didn't you join a fraternity of radio haters, start petitions, get legal and constitutional rulings? After all, this *is* a democracy.'

'And I,' said Brock, 'am that thing called a minority. I *did* join fraternities, picket, pass petitions, take it to court. Year after year I protested. Everyone laughed. Everyone else *loved* bus radios and commercials. *I* was out of step.'

'Then you should have taken it like a good soldier, don't you think? The majority rules.'

'But they went too far. If a little music and "keeping in touch" was charming, they figured a lot would be ten times as charming. I went *wild!* I got home to find my wife hysterical. *Why?* Because she had been completely out of touch with me for half a day. Remember, I did a dance on my wrist radio? Well, that night I laid plans to murder my house.'

'Are you *sure* that's how you want me to write it down?'

'That's semantically accurate. Kill it dead. It's one of those talking, singing, humming, weather-reporting, poetry-reading, novel-reciting, jingle-jangling, rockaby-crooning-when-you-go-to-bed houses. A house that screams opera to you in the shower and teaches you Spanish in your sleep. One of those blathering caves where all kinds of electronic Oracles make you feel a trifle larger than a thimble, with stoves that say, "I'm apricot pie, and I'm *done*", or "I'm prime roast beef, so *baste* me!" and other nursery gibberish like that. With beds that rock you to sleep and *shake* you awake. A house that *barely* tolerates humans, I tell you. A front door that barks: "You've mud on your feet, sir!" And an electronic vacuum hound that snuffles around after you from room to room, inhaling every fingernail or ash you drop. Jesus God, *I* say, Jesus God!'

'Quietly,' suggested the psychiatrist.

'Remember that Gilbert and Sullivan song—"I've Got It on My List, It Never Will Be Missed"? All night I listed grievances. Next morning early I bought a pistol. I *purposely* muddied my feet. I stood at our front door. The front door shrilled, "Dirty feet, muddy feet! Wipe your feet! Please be *neat!*" I shot the damn thing in its keyhole. I ran to the kitchen where the stove was just whining, "Turn me *over!*" In the middle of a mechanical omelet I did the stove to death. Oh, how it sizzled and screamed, "I'm *shorted!*" Then the telephone rang like a spoiled brat. I shoved it down the Insinkerator. I must state here and now I have *nothing* whatever against the Insinkerator; it was an innocent bystander. I feel sorry for it now, a practical device indeed, which never said a word, purred like a sleepy lion most of the time, and digested our leftovers. I'll have it restored. Then I went in and shot the televisor, that insidious beast, that Medusa, which freezes a billion people to stone every night, staring fixedly, that Siren which called and sang and promised so much and gave, after all, so little, but myself always going back, going back, hoping and waiting until—bang! Like a headless turkey, gobbling, my wife whooped out the front door. The police came. Here I *am!*'

He sat back happily and lit a cigarette.

'And did you realize, in committing these crimes, that the wrist radio, the broadcasting transmitter, the phone, the bus radio, the office intercoms, all were rented or were someone else's property?'

'I would do it all over again, so help me God.'

The psychiatrist sat there in the sunshine of that beatific smile.

'You don't want any further help from the Office of Mental Health? You're ready to take the consequences?'

'This is only the beginning,' said Mr Brock. 'I'm the vanguard of the small public which is tired of noise and being taken advantage of and pushed around and yelled at, every moment music, every moment in touch with some voice somewhere, do this, do that, quick, quick, now here, now there. You'll see. The revolt begins. My name will go down in history!'

'Mmm.' The psychiatrist seemed to be thinking.

'It'll take time, of course. It was all so enchanting at first. The very *idea* of these things, the practical uses, was wonderful. They were almost toys, to be played with, but the people got too involved, went too far, and got wrapped up in a pattern of social behaviour and couldn't get out, couldn't admit they were *in,* even. So they rationalized their nerves as something else. "Our modern age," they said. "Conditions," they said. "High-strung," they said. But mark my words, the seed has been sown. I got worldwide coverage on TV, radio, films; *there's* an irony for you. That was five days ago. A billion people know about me. Check your financial columns. Anyday now. Maybe today. Watch for a sudden spurt, a rise in sales for French chocolate icecream!'

'I see,' said the psychiatrist.

'Can I go back to my nice private cell now, where I can be alone and quiet for six months?'

'Yes,' said the psychiatrist quietly.

'Don't worry about me,' said Mr Brock, rising. 'I'm just going to sit around for a long time stuffing that nice soft bolt of quiet material in both ears.'

'Mmm,' said the psychiatrist, going to the door.

'Cheers,' said Mr Brock.

'Yes,' said the psychiatrist.

He pressed a code signal on a hidden button, the door opened, he stepped out, the door shut and locked. Alone, he moved in the offices and corridors. The first twenty yards of his walk were accompanied by 'Tambourine Chinois'. Then it was 'Tzigane', Bach's Passacaglia and Fugue in something Minor, 'Tiger Rag', 'Love is Like a Cigarette'. He took his broken wrist radio from his pocket like a dead praying mantis. He turned in at his office. A bell sounded; a voice came out of the ceiling, 'Doctor?'

'Just finished with Brock,' said the psychiatrist.

'Diagnosis?'

'Seems completely disorientated, but convivial. Refuses to accept the simplest realities of his environment and work *with* them.'

'Prognosis?'

'Indefinite. Left him enjoying a piece of invisible material.'

Three phones rang. A duplicate wrist radio in his desk drawer buzzed like a wounded grasshopper. The intercom flashed a pink light and click-clicked. Three phones rang. The drawer buzzed. Music blew in through the open door. The psychiatrist, humming quietly, fitted the new wrist radio to his wrist, flipped the intercom, talked a moment, picked up one telephone, talked, picked up another telephone, talked, picked up the third telephone, talked, touched the wrist-radio button, talked calmly and quietly, his face cool and serene, in the middle of the music and the lights flashing, the two phones ringing again, and his hands moving, and his wrist radio buzzing, and the intercoms talking, and voices speaking from the ceiling. And he went on quietly this way through the remainder of a cool, air-conditioned, and long afternoon; telephone, wrist radio, intercom, telephone, wrist radio, intercom, telephone, wrist radio, intercom, telephone, wrist radio, intercom, telephone, wrist radio, intercom, telephone, wrist radio . . .

Chronopolis

J. G. Ballard

His trial had been fixed for the next day. Exactly when, of course, neither Newman nor anyone else knew. Probably it would be during the afternoon, when the principals concerned —judge, jury and prosecutor—managed to converge on the same courtroom at the same time. With luck his defence attorney might also appear at the right moment, though the case was such an open and shut one that Newman hardly expected him to bother—besides, transport to and from the old penal complex was notoriously difficult, involved endless waiting in the grimy depot below the prison walls.

Newman had passed the time usefully. Luckily, his cell faced south and sunlight traversed it for most of the day. He divided its arc into ten equal segments, the effective daylight hours, marking the intervals with a wedge of mortar prised from the window ledge. Each segment he further subdivided into twelve smaller units.

Immediately he had a working timepiece, accurate to within virtually a minute (the final subdivision into fifths he made mentally). The sweep of white notches, curving down one wall, across the floor and metal bedstead, and up the other wall, would have been recognizable to anyone who stood with his back to the window, but no one ever did. Anyway, the guards were too stupid to understand, and the sundial had given Newman a tremendous advantage over them. Most of the time, when he wasn't recalibrating the dial, he would press against the grille, keeping an eye on the orderly room.

'Brocken!' he would shout out at 7.15, as the shadow line hit the first interval. 'Morning inspection! On your feet, man!' The sergeant would come stumbling out of his bunk in a sweat, cursing the other warders as the reveille bell split the air.

Later, Newman sang out the other events on the daily roster: roll-call, cell fatigues, breakfast, exercise and so on round to the evening roll just before dusk. Brocken regularly won the block merit for the best-run cell deck and he relied on Newman to programme the day for him, anticipate the next item on the roster and warn him if anything went on for too long—in some of the other blocks fatigues were usually over in three minutes while breakfast or exercise could go on for hours, none of the warders knowing when to stop, the prisoners insisting that they had only just begun.

Brocken never inquired how Newman organized everything so exactly; once or twice a week, when it rained or was overcast, Newman would be strangely silent, and the resulting confusion reminded the sergeant forcefully of the merits of cooperation. Newman was kept in cell privileges and all the cigarettes he needed. It was a shame that a date for the trial had finally been named.

Newman, too, was sorry. Most of his research so far had been inconclusive. Primarily his problem was that, given a northward-facing cell for the bulk of his sentence, the task of estimating the time might become impossible. The inclination of the shadows in the exercise yards or across the towers and walls provided too blunt a reading. Calibration would have to be visual; an optical instrument would soon be discovered.

What he needed was an internal timepiece, an unconsciously operating psychic mechanism regulated, say, by his pulse or respiratory rhythms. He had tried to train his time sense, running an elaborate series of tests to estimate its minimum inbuilt error, and this had been disappointingly large. The chances of conditioning an accurate reflex seemed slim.

However, unless he could tell the exact time at any given moment, he knew he would go mad.

His obsession, which now faced him with a charge of murder, had revealed itself innocently enough.

As a child, like all children, he had noticed the occasional ancient clock tower, bearing the same white circle with its twelve intervals. In the seedier areas of the city the round characteristic dials often hung over cheap jewellery stores, rusting and derelict.

'Just signs,' his mother explained. 'They don't mean anything, like stars or rings.'

Pointless embellishment, he had thought.

Once, in an old furniture shop, they had seen a clock with hands, upside down in a box full of fire-irons and miscellaneous rubbish.

'Eleven and twelve,' he had pointed out. 'What does it mean?'

His mother had hurried him away, reminding herself never to visit that street again. Time Police were still supposed to be around, watching for any outbreak. 'Nothing,' she told him sharply. 'It's all finished.' To herself she added experimentally: Five and twelve. Five *to* twelve. Yes.

Time unfolded at its usual sluggish, half-confused pace. They lived in a ramshackle house in one of the amorphous suburbs, a zone of endless afternoons. Sometimes he went to school, until he was ten spent most of his time with his mother queueing outside the closed food stores. In the evening he would play with the neighbourhood gang around the abandoned railway station, punting a home-made flat car along the overgrown tracks, or break into one of the unoccupied houses and set up a temporary command post.

He was in no hurry to grow up; the adult world was unsynchronized and ambitionless. After his mother died he spent long days in the attic, going through her trunks and old clothes, playing with the bric-à-brac of hats and beads, trying to recover something of her personality.

In the bottom compartment of her jewellery case he came across a small flat gold-cased object, equipped with a wrist strap. The dial had no hands but the twelve-numbered face intrigued him and he fastened it to his wrist.

His father choked over his soup when he saw it that evening.

'Conrad, my God! Where in heaven did you get that?'

'In Mamma's bead box. Can't I keep it?'

'No. Conrad, give it to me! Sorry, son.' Thoughtfully: 'Let's see, you're fourteen. Look, Conrad, I'll explain it all in a couple of years.'

With the impetus provided by this new taboo there was no need to wait for his father's revelations. Full knowledge came soon. The older boys knew the whole story, but strangely enough it was disappointingly dull.

'Is that all?' he kept saying. 'I don't get it. Why worry so much about clocks? We have calendars, don't we?'

Suspecting more, he scoured the streets, carefully inspecting every derelict clock for a clue to the real secret. Most of the faces had been mutilated, hands and numerals torn off, the circle of minute intervals stripped away, leaving a shadow of fading rust. Distributed apparently at random all over the city, above stores, banks and public buildings, their real purpose was hard to discover. Sure enough, they measured the progress of time through twelve arbitrary intervals, but this seemed barely adequate grounds for outlawing them. After all, a whole variety of timers were in general use: in kitchens, factories, hospitals, wherever a fixed period of time was needed. His father had one by his bed at night. Sealed into the standard small black box, and driven by miniature batteries, it emitted a high penetrating whistle shortly before breakfast the next morning, woke him if he overslept. A clock was no more than a calibrated timer, in many ways less useful, as it provided you with a steady stream of irrelevant information. What if it was half past three, as the old reckoning put it, if you weren't planning to start or finish anything then?

Making his questions sound as naïve as possible, he conducted a long, careful poll. Under fifty no one appeared to know anything at all about the historical background, and even the older people were beginning to forget. He also noticed that the less educated they were the more they were willing to talk, indicating that manual and lower-class workers had played no part in the revolution and consequently had no guilt-charged memories to repress. Old Mr Crichton, the plumber who lived in the basement apartment, reminisced without any prompting, but nothing he said threw any light on the problem.

'Sure, there were thousands of clocks then, millions of them, everybody had one. Watches we called them, strapped to the wrist, you had to screw them up every day.'

'But what did you *do* with them, Mr Crichton?' Conrad pressed.

'Well, you just — looked at them, and you knew what time it was. One o'clock, or two, or half past seven — that was when I'd go off to work.'

'But you go off to work now when you've had breakfast. And if you're late the timer rings.'

Crichton shook his head. 'I can't explain it to you, lad. You ask your father.'

But Mr Newman was hardly more helpful. The explanation promised for Conrad's sixteenth birthday never materialized. When his questions persisted Mr Newman, tired of side-stepping, shut him up with an abrupt: 'Just stop thinking about it, do you understand? You'll get yourself and the rest of us into a lot of trouble.'

Stacey, the young English teacher, had a wry sense of humour, liked to shock the boys by taking up unorthodox positions on marriage or economics. Conrad wrote an essay describing an imaginary society completely preoccupied with elaborate rituals revolving around a minute by minute observance of the passage of time.

Stacey refused to play, however, gave him a noncommittal beta plus, after class quietly asked Conrad what had prompted the fantasy. At first Conrad tried to back away, then finally came out with the question that contained the central riddle.

'Why is it against the law to have a clock?'

Stacey tossed a piece of chalk from one hand to the other.

'Is it against the law?'

Conrad nodded. 'There's an old notice in the police station offering a bounty of one hundred pounds for every clock or wristwatch brought in. I saw it yesterday. The sergeant said it was still in force.'

Stacey raised his eyebrows mockingly. 'You'll make a million. Thinking of going into business?'

Conrad ignored this. 'It's against the law to have a gun because you might shoot someone. But how can you hurt anybody with a clock?'

'Isn't it obvious? You can time him, know exactly how long it takes him to do something.'

'Well?'

'Then you can make him do it faster.'

At seventeen, on a sudden impulse, he built his first clock. Already his preoccupation with time was giving him a marked lead over his classmates. One or two were more intelligent, others more conscientious, but Conrad's ability to organize his leisure and homework periods allowed him to make the most of his talents. When the others were lounging around the railway yard on their way home Conrad had already completed half his prep, allocating his time according to its various demands.

As soon as he finished he would go up to the attic playroom, now his workshop. Here, in the old wardrobes and trunks, he made his first experimental constructions: calibrated candles, crude sundials, sand-glasses, an elaborate clockwork contraption developing about half a horse power that drove its hands progressively faster and faster in an unintentional parody of Conrad's obsession.

His first serious clock was water-powered, a slowly leaking

tank holding a wooden float that drove the hands as it sank downwards. Simple but accurate, it satisfied Conrad for several months while he carried out his everwidening search for a real clock mechanism. He soon discovered that although there were innumerable table clocks, gold pocket watches and timepieces of every variety rusting in junk shops and in the back drawers of most homes, none of them contained their mechanisms. These, together with the hands, and sometimes the digits, had always been removed. His own attempts to build an escapement that would regulate the motion of the ordinary clockwork motor met with no success; everything he had heard about clock movements confirmed that they were precision instruments of exact design and construction. To satisfy his secret ambition—a portable timepiece, if possible an actual wristwatch—he would have to find one, somewhere, in working order.

Finally, from an unexpected source, a watch came to him. One afternoon in a cinema, an elderly man sitting next to Conrad had a sudden heart attack. Conrad and two members of the audience carried him out to the manager's office. Holding one of his arms, Conrad noticed in the dim aisle light a glint of metal inside the sleeve. Quickly he felt the wrist with his fingers, identified the unmistakable lens-shaped disc of a wristwatch.

As he carried it home its tick seemed as loud as a death-knell. He clamped his hand around it, expecting everyone in the street to point accusingly at him, the Time Police to swoop down and seize him.

In the attic he took it out and examined it breathlessly, smothering it in a cushion whenever he heard his father shift about in the bedroom below. Later he realized that its noise was almost inaudible. The watch was of the same pattern as his mother's, though with a yellow and not a red face. The gold case was scratched and peeling, but the movement seemed to be in perfect condition. He prised off the rear plate, watched the frenzied flickering world of miniature cogs and wheels for hours, spellbound. Frightened of breaking the main spring, he kept the watch only half wound, packed away carefully in cotton wool.

In taking the watch from its owner he had not, in fact, been motivated by theft; his first impulse had been to hide the watch before the doctor discovered it feeling for the man's pulse. But once the watch was in his possession he abandoned any thought of tracing the owner and returning it.

That others were still wearing watches hardly surprised him. The water clock had demonstrated that a calibrated timepiece added another dimension to life, organized its energies, gave the countless activities of everyday existence a yardstick of significance. Conrad spent hours in the attic gazing at the small yellow dial, watching its minute hand revolve slowly, its hour hand press on imperceptibly, a compass charting his passage through the future. Without it he felt rudderless, adrift in a grey purposeless limbo of timeless events. His father began to seem idle and stupid, sitting around vacantly with no idea when anything was going to happen.

Soon he was wearing the watch all day. He stitched together a slim cotton sleeve, fitted with a narrow flap below which he could see the face. He timed everything—the length of classes, football games, meal breaks, the hours of daylight and darkness, sleep and waking. He amused himself endlessly by baffling his friends with demonstrations of this private sixth sense, anticipating the frequency of their heart beats, the hourly newscasts on the radio, boiling a series of identically consistent eggs without the aid of a timer.

Then he gave himself away.

Stacey, shrewder than any of the others, discovered that he was wearing a watch. Conrad had noticed that Stacey's English classes lasted exactly forty-five minutes; he let himself slide into the habit of tidying his desk a minute before Stacey's timer pipped up. Once or twice he noticed Stacey looking at him curiously, but he could not resist the temptation to impress Stacey by always being the first one to make for the door.

One day he had stacked his books and clipped away his pen when Stacey pointedly asked him to read out a précis he had done. Conrad knew the timer would pip out in less than ten seconds, and decided to sit tight and wait for the usual stampede to save him the trouble.

Stacey stepped down from the dais, waiting patiently. One or two boys turned around and frowned at Conrad, who was counting away the closing seconds.

Then, amazed, he realized that the timer had failed to sound! Panicking, he first thought his watch had broken, just restrained himself in time from looking at it.

'In a hurry, Newman?' Stacey asked dryly. He sauntered down the aisle to Conrad, smiling sardonically. Baffled, and face reddening with embarrassment, Conrad fumbled open his exercise book, read out the precis. A few minutes later, without waiting for the timer, Stacey dismissed the class.

'Newman,' he called out. 'Here a moment.'

He rummaged behind the rostrum as Conrad approached. 'What happened then?' he asked. 'Forget to wind up your watch this morning?'

Conrad said nothing. Stacey took out the timer, switched off the silencer and listened to the pip that buzzed out.

'Where did you get it from? Your parents? Don't worry, the Time Police were disbanded years ago.'

Conrad examined Stacey's face carefully. 'It was my mother's,' he lied. 'I found it among her things.' Stacey held out his hand and Conrad nervously unstrapped the watch and handed it to him.

Stacey slipped it half out of its sleeve, glanced briefly at the yellow face. 'Your mother, you say? Hmh.'

'Are you going to report me?' Conrad asked.

'What, and waste some overworked psychiatrist's time even further?'

'Isn't it breaking the law to wear a watch?'

'Well, you're not exactly the greatest living menace to public security.' Stacey started for the door, gesturing Conrad with him. He handed the watch back. 'Cancel whatever you're doing on Saturday afternoon. You and I are taking a trip.'

'Where?' Conrad asked.

'Back into the past,' Stacey said lightly. 'To Chronopolis, the Time City.'

Stacey had hired a car, a huge battered mastodon of chromium and fins. He waved jauntily to Conrad as he picked him up outside the public library.

'Climb into the turret,' he called out. He pointed to the bulging briefcase Conrad slung on to the seat between them. 'Have you had a look at those yet?'

Conrad nodded. As they moved off around the deserted square he opened the briefcase and pulled out a thick bundle of road maps. 'I've just worked out that the city covers over 500 square miles. I'd never realized it was so big. Where is everybody?'

Stacey laughed. They crossed the main street, cut down into a long tree-lined avenue of semidetached houses. Half of them were empty, windows wrecked and roofs sagging. Even the inhabited houses had a makeshift appearance, crude water towers on home-made scaffolding lashed to their chimneys, piles of logs dumped in overgrown front gardens.

'Thirty million people once lived in this city,' Stacey remarked. 'Now the population is little more than two, and still declining. Those of us left hang on in what were once the distal suburbs, so that the city today is effectively an enormous ring, five miles in width, encircling a vast dead centre forty or fifty miles in diameter.'

They wove in and out of various back roads, past a small factory still running although work was supposed to end at noon, finally picked up a long, straight boulevard that carried them steadily westwards. Conrad traced their progress across successive maps. They were nearing the edge of the annulus Stacey had described. On the map it was overprinted in green

78

so that the central interior appeared a flat, uncharted grey, a massive *terra incognita.*

They passed the last of the small shopping thoroughfares he remembered, a frontier post of mean terraced houses, dismal streets spanned by massive steel viaducts. Stacey pointed up at one as they drove below it. 'Part of the elaborate railway system that once existed, an enormous network of stations and junctions that carried fifteen million people into a dozen great terminals every day.'

For half an hour they drove on, Conrad hunched against the window, Stacey watching him in the driving mirror. Gradually, the landscape began to change. The houses were taller, with coloured roofs, the sidewalks were railed off and fitted with pedestrian lights and turnstiles. They had entered the inner suburbs, completely deserted streets with multilevel supermarkets, towering cinemas and department stores.

Chin in one hand, Conrad stared out silently. Lacking any means of transport he had never ventured into the uninhabited interior of the city, like the other children always headed in the opposite direction for the open country. Here the streets had died twenty or thirty years earlier; plate-glass shopfronts had slipped and smashed into the roadway, old neon signs, window frames and overhead wires hung down from every cornice, trailing a ragged webwork of disintegrating metal across the pavements. Stacey drove slowly, avoiding the occasional bus or truck abandoned in the middle of the road, its tyres peeling off their rims.

Conrad craned up at the empty windows, into the narrow alleys and sidestreets, but nowhere felt any sensation of fear or anticipation. These streets were merely derelict, as un-haunted as a half-empty dustbin.

One suburban centre gave way to another, to long intervening stretches of congested ribbon developments. Mile by mile, the architecture altered its character; buildings were larger, ten- or fifteen-storey blocks, clad in facing materials of green and blue tiles, glass or copper sheathing.

They were moving forward in time rather than, as Conrad had expected, back into the past of a fossil city.

Stacey worked the car through a nexus of sidestreets towards a six-lane expressway that rose on tall concrete buttresses above the rooftops. They found a side road that circled up to it, levelled out and then picked up speed sharply, spinning along one of the clear centre lanes.

Conrad craned forward. In the distance, two or three miles away, the tall rectilinear outlines of enormous apartment blocks reared up thirty or forty storeys high, hundreds of them lined shoulder to shoulder in apparently endless ranks, like giant dominoes.

'We're entering the central dormitories here,' Stacey told him. On either side buildings overtopped the motorway, the congestion mounting so that some of them had been built right up against the concrete palisades.

In a few minutes they passed between the first of the apartment batteries, the thousands of identical living units with their slanting balconies shearing up into the sky, the glass in-falls of the aluminium curtain walling speckling in the sunlight. The smaller houses and shops of the outer suburbs had vanished. There was no room on the ground level. In the narrow intervals between the blocks there were small concrete gardens, shopping complexes, ramps banking down into huge underground car parks.

And on all sides there were the clocks. Conrad noticed them immediately, at every street corner, over every archway, three-quarters of the way up the sides of buildings, covering every conceivable angle of approach. Most of them were too high off the ground to be reached by anything less than a fireman's ladder and still retained their hands. All registered the same time: 12.01.

Conrad looked at his wrist-watch, noted that it was just 2.45 pm.

'They were driven by a master clock,' Stacey told him. 'When that stopped they all seized at the same moment. One minute after midnight, thirty-seven years ago.'

The afternoon had darkened, as the high cliffs cut off the sunlight, the sky a succession of narrow vertical intervals opening and closing around them. Down on the canyon floor it was dismal and oppressive, a wilderness of concrete and frosted glass. The expressway divided and pressed on westwards. After a few more miles the apartment blocks gave way to the first office buildings in the central zone. These were even taller, sixty or seventy storeys high, linked by spiralling ramps and causeways. The expressway was fifty feet off the ground yet the first floors of the office blocks were level with it, mounted on massive stilts that straddled the glass-enclosed entrance bays of lifts and escalators. The streets were wide but featureless. The sidewalks of parallel roadways merged below the buildings, forming a continuous concrete apron. Here and there were the remains of cigarette kiosks, rusting stairways up to restaurants and arcades built on platforms thirty feet in the air.

Conrad, however, was looking only at the clocks. Never had he visualized so many, in places so dense that they obscured each other. Their faces were multicoloured: red, blue, yellow, green. Most of them carried four or five hands. Although the master hands had stopped at a minute past twelve, the subsidiary hands had halted at varying positions, apparently dictated by their colour.

'What were the extra hands for?' he asked Stacey. 'And the different colours?'

'Time zones. Depending on your professional category and the consumer-shifts allowed. Hold on, though, we're almost there.'

They left the expressway and swung off down a ramp that fed them into the north-east corner of a wide open plaza, eight hundred yards long and half as wide, down the centre of which had once been laid a continuous strip of lawn, now rank and overgrown. The plaza was empty, a sudden block of free space bounded by tall glass-faced cliffs that seemed to carry the sky.

Stacey parked, and he and Conrad climbed out and stretched themselves. Together they strolled across the wide pavement towards the strip of waist-high vegetation. Looking down the vistas receding from the plaza Conrad grasped fully for the first time the vast perspectives of the city, the massive geometric jungle of buildings.

Stacey put one foot up on the balustrade running around the lawn bed, pointed to the far end of the plaza, where Conrad saw a low-lying huddle of buildings of unusual architectural style, nineteenth-century perpendicular, stained by the atmosphere and badly holed by a number of explosions. Again, however, his attention was held by the clock face built into a tall concrete tower just behind the older buildings. This was the largest clock dial he had ever seen, at least a hundred feet across, huge black hands halted at a minute past twelve. The dial was white, the first they had seen, but on wide semicircular shoulders built out off the tower below the main face were a dozen smaller faces, no more than twenty feet in diameter, running the full spectrum of colours. Each had five hands, the inferior three halted at random.

'Fifty years ago,' Stacey explained, gesturing at the ruins below the tower, 'that collection of ancient buildings was one of the world's greatest legislative assemblies.' He gazed at it quietly for a few moments, then turned to Conrad. 'Enjoy the ride?'

Conrad nodded fervently. 'It's impressive, all right. The people who lived here must have been giants. What's really remarkable is that it looks as if they left only yesterday. Why don't we go back?'

'Well, apart from the fact that there aren't enough of us now, even if there were we couldn't control it. In its heyday this city was a fantastically complex social organism. The communications problems are difficult to imagine merely by looking at these blank façades. It's the tragedy of this city that there appeared to be only one way to solve them.'

'Did they solve them?'

'Oh, yes, certainly. But they left themselves out of the

equation. Think of the problems, though. Transporting fifteen million office workers to and from the centre every day, routeing in an endless stream of cars, buses, trains, helicopters, linking every office, almost every desk, with a videophone, every apartment with television, radio, power, water, feeding and entertaining this enormous number of people, guarding them with ancillary services, police, fire squads, medical units—it all hinged on one factor.'

Stacey threw a fist out at the great tower clock. 'Time! Only by synchronizing every activity, every footstep forward or backward, every meal, bus-halt, and telephone call, could the organism support itself. Like the cells in your body, which proliferate into mortal cancers if allowed to grow in freedom, every individual here had to subserve the overriding needs of the city or fatal bottlenecks threw it into total chaos. You and I can turn on the tap any hour of the day or night, because we have our own private water cisterns, but what would happen here if everybody washed the breakfast dishes within the same ten minutes?'

They began to walk slowly down the plaza towards the clock tower. 'Fifty years ago, when the population was only ten million, they could just provide for a potential peak capacity, but even then a strike in one essential service paralysed most of the others; it took workers two or three hours to reach their offices, as long again to queue for lunch and get home. As the population climbed the first serious attempts were made to stagger hours; workers in certain areas started the day an hour earlier or later than those in others. Their railway passes and car number plates were coloured accordingly, and if they tried to travel outside the permitted periods they were turned back. Soon the practice spread; you could only switch on your washing-machine at a given hour, post a letter or take a bath at a specific period.'

'Sounds feasible,' Conrad commented, his interest mounting. 'But how did they enforce all this?'

'By a system of coloured passes, coloured money, an elaborate set of schedules published every day like the TV or radio programmes. And, of course, by all the thousands of clocks you can see around you here. The subsidiary hands marked out the number of minutes remaining in any activity period for people in the clock's colour category.'

Stacey stopped, pointed to a blue-faced clock mounted on one of the buildings overlooking the plaza. 'Let's say, for example, that a lower-grade executive leaving his office at the allotted time, twelve o'clock, wants to have lunch, change a library book, buy some aspirin, and telephone his wife. Like all executives, his identity zone is blue. He takes out his schedule for the week, or looks down the blue-time columns in the newspaper, and notes that his lunch period for that day is 12.15 to 12.30. He has fifteen minutes to kill. Right, he then checks the library. Time code for today is given as 3, that's the third hand on the clock. He looks at the nearest blue clock, the third hand says 37 minutes past—he has twenty-three minutes, ample time, to reach the library. He starts down the street, but finds at the first intersection that the pedestrian lights are only shining red and green and he can't get across. The area's been temporarily zoned off for lower-grade women office workers—red, and manuals—greens.'

'What would happen if he ignored the lights?' Conrad asked.

'Nothing immediately, but all blue clocks in the zoned area would have returned to zero, and no shops or the library would serve him, unless he happened to have red or green currency and a forged set of library tickets. Anyway, the penalties were too high to make the risk worthwhile, and the whole system was evolved for his convenience, no one else's. So, unable to reach the library, he decides on the chemist. The time code for the chemist is five, the fifth, smallest hand. It reads 54 minutes past: he has six minutes to find a chemist and make his purchase. This done, he still has five minutes before lunch, decides to phone his wife. Checking the phone code he sees that no period has been provided for private calls that day—or the next. He'll just have to wait until he sees her that evening.'

'What if he did phone?'

'He wouldn't be able to get his money in the coin box, and even then, his wife, assuming she is a secretary, would be in a red time zone and no longer in her office for that day—hence the prohibition on phone calls. It all meshed perfectly. Your time programme told you when you could switch on your TV set and when to switch off. All electric appliances were fused, and if you strayed outside the programmed periods you'd have a hefty fine and repair bill to meet. The viewer's economic status obviously determined the choice of programme, and vice versa, so there was no question of coercion. Each day's programme listed your permitted activities: you could go to the hairdresser's, cinema, bank, cocktail bar, at stated times, and if you went then you were sure of being served quickly and efficiently.'

They had almost reached the far end of the plaza. Facing them on its tower was the enormous clock face, dominating its constellation of twelve motionless attendants.

'There were a dozen socioeconomic categories: blue for executives, gold for professional classes, yellow for military and government officials—incidentally, it's odd your parents ever got hold of that wristwatch, none of your family ever worked for the government—green for manual workers and so on. But, naturally, subtle subdivisions were possible. The lower-grade executive I mentioned left his office at 12, but a senior executive, with exactly the same time codes, would leave at 11.45, have an extra fifteen minutes, would find the streets clear before the lunch-hour rush of clerical workers.'

Stacey pointed up at the tower. 'This was the Big Clock, the master from which all others were regulated. Central Time Control, a sort of Ministry of Time, gradually took over the old parliamentary buildings as their legislative functions diminished. The programmers were, effectively, the city's absolute rulers.'

As Stacey continued Conrad gazed up at the battery of timepieces, poised helplessly at 12.01. Somehow time itself seemed to have been suspended, around him the great office buildings hung in a neutral interval between yesterday and tomorrow. If one could only start the master clock the entire city would probably slide into gear and come to life, in an instant be repeopled with its dynamic jostling millions.

They began to walk back towards the car. Conrad looked over his shoulder at the clock face, its gigantic arms upright on the silent hour.

'Why did it stop?' he asked.

Stacey looked at him curiously. 'Haven't I made it fairly plain?'

'What do you mean?' Conrad pulled his eyes off the scores of clocks lining the plaza, frowned at Stacey.

'Can you imagine what life was like for all but a few of the thirty million people here?'

Conrad shrugged. Blue and yellow clocks, he noticed, outnumbered all others; obviously the major governmental agencies had operated from the plaza area. 'Highly organized but better than the sort of life we lead,' he replied finally, more interested in the sights around him. 'I'd rather have the telephone for one hour a day than not at all. Scarcities are always rationed, aren't they?'

'But this was a way of life in which everything was scarce. Don't you think there's a point beyond which human dignity is surrendered?'

Conrad snorted. 'There seems to be plenty of dignity here. Look at these buildings, they'll stand for a thousand years. Try comparing them with my father. Anyway, think of the beauty of the system, engineered as precisely as a watch.'

'That's all it was,' Stacey commented dourly. 'The old metaphor of the cog in the wheel was never more true than here. The full sum of your existence was printed for you in the newspaper columns, mailed to you once a month from the Ministry of Time.'

Conrad was looking off in some other direction and Stacey pressed on in a slightly louder voice. 'Eventually, of course, revolt came. It's interesting that in any industrial society there is usually one social revolution each century, and that successive revolutions receive their impetus from progressively higher social levels. In the eighteenth century it was the urban proletariat, in the nineteenth the artisan classes, in this revolt the white collar office worker, living in his tiny so-called modern flat, supporting through credit pyramids an economic system that denied him all freedom of will or personality, chained him to a thousand clocks. . . . ' He broke off. 'What's the matter?'

Conrad was staring down one of the sidestreets. He hesitated, then asked in a casual voice: 'How were these clocks driven? Electrically?'

'Most of them. A few mechanically. Why?'

'I just wondered . . . how they kept them all going.' He dawdled at Stacey's heels, checking the time from his wristwatch and glancing to his left. There were twenty or thirty clocks hanging from the buildings along the sidestreet, indistinguishable from those he had seen all afternoon.

Except for the fact that one of them was working!

It was mounted in the centre of a black glass portico over an entrance-way fifty yards down the right-hand side, about eighteen inches in diameter, with a faded blue face. Unlike the others its hands registered 3.15, the correct time. Conrad had nearly mentioned this apparent coincidence to Stacey when he had suddenly seen the minute hand move on an interval. Without doubt someone had restarted the clock; even if it had been running off an inexhaustible battery, after thirty-seven years it could never have displayed such accuracy.

He hung behind Stacey, who was saying: 'Every revolution had its symbol of oppression. . . . '

The clock was almost out of view. Conrad was about to bend down and tie his shoelace when he saw the minute hand jerk downwards, tilt slightly from the horizontal.

He followed Stacey towards the car, no longer bothering to listen to him. Ten yards from it he turned and broke away, ran swiftly across the roadway towards the nearest building.

'Newman!' he heard Stacey shout. 'Come back!' He reachcd the pavement, ran between the great concrete pillars carrying the building. He paused for a moment behind an elevator shaft, saw Stacey climbing hurriedly into the car. The engine coughed and roared out, and Conrad sprinted on below the building into a rear alley that led back to the sidestreet. Behind him he heard the car accelerating, a door slam as it picked up speed.

When he entered the sidestreet the car came swinging off the plaza thirty yards behind him. Stacey swerved off the roadway, bumped up on to the pavement and gunned the car towards Conrad, throwing on the brakes in savage lurches, blasting the horn in an attempt to frighten him. Conrad sidestepped out of its way, almost falling over the bonnet, hurled himself up a narrow stairway leading to the first floor and raced up the steps to a short landing that ended in tall glass doors. Through them he could see a wide balcony that ringed the building. A fire-escape crisscrossed upwards to the roof, giving way on the fifth floor to a cafeteria that spanned the street to the office building opposite.

Below he heard Stacey's feet running across the pavement. The glass doors were locked. He pulled a fire-extinguisher from its bracket, tossed the heavy cylinder against the centre of the plate. The glass slipped and crashed to the tiled floor in a sudden cascade, splashing down the steps. Conrad stepped through on to the balcony, began to climb the stairway. He had reached the third floor when he saw Stacey below, craning upwards. Hand over hand, Conrad pulled himself up the next two flights, swung over a bolted metal turnstile into the open court of the cafeteria. Tables and chairs lay about on their sides, mixed up with the splintered remains of desks thrown down from the upper floors.

The doors into the covered restaurant were open, a large pool of water lying across the floor. Conrad splashed through it, went over to a window and peered down past an old plastic plant into the street. Stacey seemed to have given up. Conrad crossed the rear of the restaurant, straddled the counter and climbed through a window on to the open terrace running across the street. Beyond the rail he could see into the plaza, the double line of tyre marks curving into the street below.

He had almost crossed to the opposite balcony when a shot roared out into the air. There was a sharp tinkle of falling glass and the sound of the explosion boomed away among the empty canyons.

For a few seconds he panicked. He flinched back from the exposed rail, his eardrums numbed, looking up at the great rectangular masses towering above him on either side, the endless tiers of windows like the faceted eyes of gigantic insects. So Stacey had been armed, almost certainly was a member of the Time Police!

On his hands and knees Conrad scurried along the terrace, slid through the turnstiles and headed for a half-open window on the balcony.

Climbing through, he quickly lost himself in the building.

He finally took up a position in a corner office on the sixth floor, the cafeteria just below him to the right, the stairway up which he had escaped directly opposite.

All afternoon Stacey drove up and down the adjacent streets, sometimes free-wheeling silently with the engine off, at others blazing through at speed. Twice he fired into the air, stopping the car afterwards to call out, his words lost among the echoes rolling from one street to the next. Often he drove along the pavements, swerved about below the buildings as if he expected to flush Conrad from behind one of the banks of escalators.

Finally he appeared to drive off for good, and Conrad turned his attention to the clock in the portico. It had moved on to 6.45, almost exactly the time given by his own watch. Conrad reset this to what he assumed was the correct time, then sat back and waited for whoever had wound it to appear. Around him the thirty or forty other clocks he could see remained stationary at 12.01.

For five minutes he left his vigil, scooped some water off the pool in the cafeteria, suppressed his hunger and shortly after midnight fell asleep in a corner behind the desk.

He woke the next morning to bright sunlight flooding into the office. Standing up, he dusted his clothes, turned around to find a small grey-haired man in a patched tweed suit surveying him with sharp eyes. Slung in the crook of his arm was a large black-barrelled weapon, its hammers menacingly cocked.

The man put down a steel ruler he had evidently tapped against a cabinet, waited for Conrad to collect himself.

'What are you doing here?' he asked in a testy voice. Conrad noticed his pockets were bulging with angular objects that weighed down the sides of his jacket.

'I . . . er . . .' Conrad searched for something to say. Something about the old man convinced him that this was the clock-winder. Suddenly he decided he had nothing to lose by being frank, and blurted out: 'I saw the clock working. Down there on the left. I want to help wind them all up again.'

The old man watched him shrewdly. He had an alert bird-like face, twin folds under his chin like a cockerel's.

'How do you propose to do that?' he asked.

Stuck by this one, Conrad said lamely: 'I'd find a key somewhere.'

The old man frowned. 'One key? That wouldn't do much good.' He seemed to be relaxing slowly, shook his pockets with a dull chink.

For a few moments neither of them said anything. Then Conrad had an inspiration, bared his wrist. 'I have a watch, he said. 'It's 7.45.'

'Let me see.' The old man stepped forward, briskly took Conrad's wrist, examined the yellow dial. 'Movado Supermatic,' he said to himself. 'CTC issue.' He stepped back lowering the shotgun, seemed to be summing Conrad up. 'Good,' he remarked at last. 'Let's see. You probably need some breakfast.'

They made their way out of the building, began to walk quickly down the street.

'People sometimes come here,' the old man said. 'Sightseers and police. I watched your escape yesterday, you were lucky

90

not to be killed.' They swerved left and right across the empty streets, the old man darting between the stairways and buttresses. As he walked he held his hands stiffly to his sides, preventing his pockets from swinging. Glancing into them, Conrad saw that they were full of keys, large and rusty, of every design and combination.

'I presume that was your father's watch,' the old man remarked.

'Grandfather's,' Conrad corrected. He remembered Stacey's lecture, and added: 'He was killed in the plaza.'

The old man frowned sympathetically, for a moment held Conrad's arm.

They stopped below a building, indistinguishable from the others nearby, at one time a bank. The old man looked carefully around him, eyeing the high cliff walls on all sides, then led the way up a stationary escalator.

His quarters were on the second floor, beyond a maze of steel grilles and strongdoors, a stove and a hammock slung in the centre of a large workshop. Lying about on thirty or forty desks in what had once been a typing pool, was an enormous collection of clocks, all being simultaneously repaired. Tall cabinets surrounded them, loaded with thousands of spare parts in neatly labelled correspondence trays— escapements, ratchets, cogwheels, barely recognizable through the rust.

The old man led Conrad over to a wall chart, pointed to the total listed against a column of dates. 'Look at this. There are now 278 running continuously. Believe me, I'm glad you've come. It takes me half my time to keep them wound.'

He made breakfast for Conrad, told him something about himself. His name was Marshall. Once he had worked in Central Time Control as a programmer, had survived the revolt and the Time Police, ten years later returned to the city. At the beginning of each month he cycled out to one of the perimeter towns to cash his pension and collect supplies. The rest of the time he spent winding the steadily increasing number of functioning clocks and searching for others he could dismantle and repair.

'All these years in the rain hasn't done them any good,' he explained, 'and there's nothing I can do with the electrical ones.'

Conrad wandered off among the desks, gingerly feeling the dismembered timepieces that lay around like the nerve cells of some vast unimaginable robot. He felt exhilarated and yet at the same time curiously calm, like a man who has staked his whole life on the turn of a wheel and is waiting for it to spin.

'How can you make sure that they all tell the same time?' he asked Marshall, wondering why the question seemed so important.

Marshall gestured irritably. 'I can't, but what does it matter? There is no such thing as a perfectly accurate clock. The nearest you can get is one that has stopped. Although you never know when, it *is* absolutely accurate twice a day.'

Conrad went over to the window, pointed to the great clock visible in an interval between the rooftops. 'If only we could start that, and run all the others off it.'

'Impossible. The entire mechanism was dynamited. Only the chimer is intact. Anyway, the wiring of the electrically-driven clocks perished years ago. It would take an army of engineers to recondition them.'

Conrad nodded, looked at the scoreboard again. He noticed that Marshall appeared to have lost his way through the years—the completion dates he listed were seven and a half years out. Idly, Conrad reflected on the significance of this irony, but decided not to mention it to Marshall.

For three months Conrad lived with the old man, following him on foot as he cycled about on his rounds, carrying the ladder and the satchel full of keys with which Marshall wound up the clocks, helping him to dismantle recoverable ones and carry them back to the workshop. All day, and often through half the night, they worked together, repairing the movements, restarting the clocks and returning them to their original positions.

All the while, however, Conrad's mind was fixed upon the great clock in its tower dominating the plaza. Once a day he managed to sneak off and make his way into the ruined Time buildings. As Marshall had said, neither the clock nor its twelve satellites would ever run again. The movement house looked like the engine-room of a sunken ship, a rusting tangle of rotors and drive wheels exploded into contorted shapes. Every week he would climb the long stairway up to the topmost platform two hundred feet above, look out through the bell tower at the flat roofs of the office blocks stretching away to the horizon. The hammers rested against their trips in long ranks just below him. Once he kicked one of the treble trips playfully, sent a dull chime out across the plaza.

The sound drove strange echoes into his mind.

Slowly he began to repair the chimer mechanism, rewiring the hammers and the pulley systems, trailing fresh wire up the great height of the tower, dismantling the winches in the movement room below and renovating their clutches.

He and Marshall never discussed their self-appointed tasks. Like animals obeying an instinct they worked tirelessly, barely aware of their own motives. When Conrad told him one day that he intended to leave and continue the work in another sector of the city, Marshall agreed immediately, gave Conrad as many tools as he could spare and bade him goodbye.

Six months later, almost to the day, the sounds of the great clock chimed out across the rooftops of the city, marking the hours, the half-hours and the quarter-hours, steadily tolling the progress of the day. Thirty miles away, in the towns forming the perimeter of the city, people stopped in the streets and in doorways, listening to the dim haunted echoes reflected through the long aisles of apartment blocks on the far horizon, involuntarily counting the slow final sequences that told the hour. Older people whispered to each other: 'Four o'clock, or was it five? They have started the clock again. It seems strange after these years.'

And all through the day they would pause as the quarter and half hours reached across the miles to them, a voice from their childhoods reminding them of the ordered world of the past. They began to reset their timers by the chimes, at night before they slept they would listen to the long count of midnight, wake to hear them again in the thin clear air of the morning.

Some went down to the police station and asked if they could have their watches and clocks back again.

After sentence, twenty years for the murder of Stacey, five for fourteen offences under the Time Laws, to run concurrently, Newman was led away to the holding cells in the basement of the court. He had expected the sentence and made no comment when invited by the judge. After waiting trial for a year the afternoon in the courtroom was nothing more than a momentary intermission.

He made no attempt to defend himself against the charge of killing Stacey, partly to shield Marshall, who would be able to continue their work unmolested, and partly because he felt indirectly responsible for the policeman's death. Stacey's body, skull fractured by a twenty- or thirty-storey fall, had been discovered in the back seat of his car in a basement garage not far from the plaza. Presumably Marshall had discovered him prowling around and dealt with him single-handed. Newman recalled that one day Marshall had disappeared altogether and had been curiously irritable for the rest of the week.

The last time he had seen the old man had been during the three days before the police arrived. Each morning as the chimes boomed out across the plaza Newman had seen his tiny figure striding briskly down the plaza towards him, waving up energetically at the tower, bareheaded and unafraid.

Now Newman was faced with the problem of how to devise a clock that would chart his way through the coming twenty years. His fears increased when he was taken the next day to the cell block which housed the long-term prisoners — passing his cell on the way to meet the superintendent he noticed that his window looked out on to a small shaft. He pumped his brains desperately as he stood to attention during the superintendent's homilies, wondering how he could retain his sanity. Short of counting the seconds, each one of the 86,400 in every day, he saw no possible means of assessing the time.

Locked into his cell, he sat limply on the narrow bed, too tired to unpack his small bundle of possessions. A moment's inspection confirmed the uselessness of the shaft. A powerful light mounted half-way up masked the sunlight that slipped through a steel grille fifty feet above.

He stretched himself out on the bed and examined the ceiling. A lamp was recessed into its centre, but a second, surprisingly, appeared to have been fitted to the cell. This was on the wall, a few feet above his head. He could see the curving bowl of the protective case, some ten inches in diameter.

He was wondering whether this could be a reading light when he realized that there was no switch.

Swinging round, he sat up and examined it, then leapt to his feet in astonishment.

It was a clock! He pressed his hands against the bowl, reading the circle of numerals, noting the inclination of the hands. 4.53, near enough the present time. Not simply a clock, but one in running order! Was this some sort of macabre joke, or a misguided attempt at rehabilitation?

His pounding on the door brought a warder.

'What's all the noise about? The clock? What's the matter with it?' He unlocked the door and barged in, pushing Newman back.

'Nothing. But why is it here? They're against the law.'

'Oh, is that what's worrying you.' The warder shrugged. 'Well, you see, the rules are a little different in here. You lads have got a lot of time ahead of you, it'd be cruel not to let you know where you stood. You know how to work it, do you? Good.' He slammed the door, bolted it fast, smiled at Newman through the cage. 'It's a long day here, son, as you'll be finding out, that'll help you get through it.'

Gleefully, Newman lay on the bed, his head on a rolled blanket at its foot, staring up at the clock. It appeared to be in perfect order, electrically driven, moving in rigid half-minute jerks. For an hour after the warder left he watched it without a break, then began to tidy up his cell, glancing over his shoulder every few minutes to reassure himself that it was still there, still running efficiently. The irony of the situation, the total inversion of justice, delighted him, even though it would cost him twenty years of his life.

He was still chuckling over the absurdity of it all two weeks later when for the first time he noticed the clock's insanely irritating tick . . . .

The Man who Rode the Saucer

Kenyon Holmes

The intercommunicating system flashed my number. I turned it on and got the boss's secretary.

'Mr Martin, Mr Tralor wants to see you.'

'I'm in the middle of the Lessing story,' I said.

'Now,' she said.

I got up and went into the city editor's office. He looked harassed, but that was natural; his hair was always tousled, his shirt-sleeves were always rolled up, his vest was always either open all the way or cast aside. This morning it was open.

'Got an assignment for you, Martin,' he said. 'I'm afraid it's another saucer story.'

'My God!' I protested.

'Sure, say it, I know! I'm fed up to the gills on flying saucers, but we can't very well ignore this one. It comes from Professor Ford Massingham.'

'Don't tell me he's seen a flying saucer.'

Tralor shook his massive head. 'I wish he had. No, it's not that. It's a colleague of his. He had the story from him; he thinks we should get it from him, too. Henry Creigh, 77 West Malden.'

'That's the same fellow who was missing for a week last month,' I said.

Tralor nodded. 'That's it. Circumstantial evidence. We had the story about his turning up "in a dazed condition". The usual "amnesia" case. Now it turns out that's the story he fed us; he told his colleagues at the university, where he was teaching—he's home now, off the staff—an entirely different story.'

Tralor looked at me a little queerly; I felt a kind of apprehension at the base of my spine, travelling upwards.

'Don't tell me,' I said. 'He saw a flying saucer.'

'He did better than that,' answered Tralor. 'He took a ride on one.'

'Now I've heard everything,' I said.

'Get the story from him. Maybe we can do a feature on the man who rode the saucer. But I don't know. Let's see what you can get. Turn the Lessing story over to Baird; he can handle it.'

I took a cab out to the address on West Malden. It was a neat, bungalow-type house, about ten years old, maybe less. It looked modern. A pert young woman answered the door and stood barring my way. I introduced myself.

'Look, Mr Martin,' she said, having identified herself as Creigh's daughter, 'it's no use. My father isn't well; he isn't seeing anyone.'

'If he did what he said he did, it's news,' I said. 'More than that, it's important to the nation, maybe the world. Who knows? I've got to see him.'

'To tell the truth, nobody knows whether he's going to live or die,' she went on coldly. 'He's kept in a darkened room, and he doesn't want to see anyone; we respect his wishes.'

'Will you do this for me? Will you tell him Professor Massingham sent me?'

She hesitated at that, but at last said, 'Wait here,' and went off to talk to her father.

It worked. She came back, gave me a glance that might have meant anything, and said, 'Come along. He'll ring the bell for me when he wants you to go. Please don't try to stop him; it might be unpleasant.'

It was on the tip of my tongue to say that I was used to unpleasant things, but I held it back in time.

Creigh was in a darkened room, all right. It was darker than dark. His daughter had one of those pencil-point flashlights. She led me in with that, flashed it on a chair at her father's bedside, and put the light briefly on her father's face. It was an odd, curiously coloured face—maroon, I thought, or mauve; it startled me. It was long, drawn, and it seemed in the brief glance I had of it horribly out of proportion, as if someone had taken it and remoulded and stretched it. The eyes were haunting.

'Mr Martin,' he said. 'You may go, Cissie.'

The light went out; his daughter left the room.

'I'm sorry to barge in like this, Mr Creigh,' I said. 'But Professor Massingham thought someone should take down your story for posterity. I got the assignment.'

'I see. The impartial, nonscientific observer. That is symptomatic of our American civilization, Mr Martin.'

'We've had all kinds of reports of flying saucers being seen. But this is something new. They tell me you rode a flying saucer.'

'I did.'

He was reluctant to talk about it, but it came out, bit by bit. In the beginning, the story was pretty much like most of the others. He had been out on a field trip, alone. No corroborative evidence in that, of course. He had been looking over some shale when he heard a humming noise quite close by. He looked up, and saw the saucer. It was just completing an arc-like descending swing, and even as he watched, it came down like a feather about thirty yards or so from him. There it rested.

'It was about the shape of a flat-headed top; "saucer" described it very well. Its diameter was probably a hundred feet, but it was deep enough: forty feet or so. It wasn't perfectly smooth—there were appendages—some sort of landing gear, not wheels, but something, I found out later, that worked on the principle of the electric eye. There were appendages at the top and down the near side, too, with the look of having been made for climbing. It was of a kind of metal that had no similarity to anything I knew.'

The saucer had simply rested there. Nothing had come out of it. There had been no sign of life about it. Creigh had finally overcome his astonishment sufficiently to let his curiosity take over. He left his paraphernalia where he stood and went cautiously over to the saucer. Judging that its entrance lay on its top side, he took hold of the projections and began to climb. There was a kind of hatchway at the top, but nothing to show how it would open. While he was topside, the saucer began to move.

'As a matter of fact, I didn't notice it at first. The thing just rose up like a helicopter and, before I knew it, we were a couple hundred feet off the ground. I had to hang on to the projections, for the saucer was increasing speed rapidly. We went up quite far and drove northwest. I was lying on the hatch, with a leg wound around one of the projections and hanging on to two others. I knew I couldn't hold out long. We had gone perhaps twenty miles, as the crow flies, when the hatch began to lower; I went with it, still hanging on. But at last I had to let go; I dropped in, rolled off the hatch, and found myself inside.'

'What did you find there?' I asked.

'Nothing. I lost consciousness.'

When he came to, he was still in the saucer, which was now at a high altitude and driving along at a very great speed. Supersonic? He could not say. He was in a compartment of the saucer; there were manifestly other compartments and guiding intelligences were in at least one of them because he caught a glimpse of someone looking in at him through what appeared to be a glass screen in one wall of his compartment.

'What sort of "someone"?' I asked.

'I thought at first it was someone human. I found out later it wasn't,' said Creigh. 'But small—half my size.'

'That would make him a midget.'

'Well, in a sense, they all were. Manlike. But not men, no. Still, there was a kinship. In another climate, on another planet, in other circumstances, man might have evolved like that. You would be as hard put to it to imagine their kind as I was to accept them—a cross between men and insects. Their arms and legs were insect-like; they had two legs and six arms, if you could call them that—hard, bone-like projections, and their heads were elongated and had certain rudimentary appendages, similar to antennae. And their colour—they were maroon.'

'You said "all". Did you see more than one?'

'That was later. After we landed. Things had happened to me by that time.'

He explained that he had been given a bath in some sort of ray which had the effect of immunizing him against heat or cold. For they came down in a place which had no resemblance to Earth, and yet it was Earth, of course. Hot by day, cold by night. Creigh's guess was a remote corner of the Gobi desert.

There were caverns, a subterranean settlement, a replica of an explorer's camp, set up for a temporary stay only as a base of operations. There were half a dozen of the saucers in evidence, and the place swarmed with the curious manlike insects—or insect-like men—all going about tasks with the precision of ants. The central building was a sort of intelligence bureau combined with a laboratory, to which they took Creigh.

'I could see at a glance that they were busy analysing geological and entomological specimens, dissecting birds and animals, making charts of a clearly anthropological nature. In short, the entire appearance of the extensive laboratory, which had the look of having been put together with some kind of plastic material to serve only temporarily, suggested that a thoroughgoing examination of the planet and its habitants was in progress. To that end, apparently, I could be of service.

'They took me into the laboratory and it was perfectly plain that my capture excited some of the scientists—I suppose, in their own terms, they had a right to be called that. Certainly the appearance of the major Earth mammal was familiar enough to the pilots of the saucers, but to the laboratory-bound scientists a creature so closely resembling themselves must have seemed a fortunate discovery indeed.

'They got to work on me at once.'

Creigh had been semistuporized and made helpless. There was evidently no intention to harm him. He was given some kind of drug resembling scopolamine, and he talked freely. His interrogators were patently delighted to discover that he was, like them, a scientist. He could not understand their language, which seemed oddly dissonant and stridulant, but he nevertheless appeared to answer their questions in a general manner, and they understood him. They had a certain rudimentary knowledge of English, as well as of some other languages — in their attempts to talk with him, they used Spanish, German, and French phrases and words. In turn, they gave him certain information, both directly and by inference.

They were representatives of an alien culture, all right. Not Martians—the wild guess some newspapers had made about the pilots of the flying saucers—not Venusians; they were from considerably more distant regions. A neighbouring galaxy, with their own sun and its planets, from a star which, as closely as Creigh could estimate, must have been within the orbit of Antares, their sun. They had examined several of Earth's sister planets and found them unsuitable for their colonization; Earth, however, appeared to be more promising, and the incidence of mankind on its surface offered exciting possibilities. They were not a large race, there were probably not more than fifty million of them, all told. But all highly developed, long past an atomic age. In certain respects, indeed, a good many, Earthmen were considerably lagging by comparison.

'I interposed objections. How could they hope for mastery of Earth? They were not looking for mastery, but only for living space. *Lebensraum*. I had heard that before; all of us have. Moreover, they could live on equal terms with men, impart their scientific knowledge, accept in return such terrene knowledge as they lacked. They could expect to assimilate Earthmen or be assimilated by mankind.

'I questioned that. Their reply was confident. Had our

various races not become amalgamated through interbreeding? Clearly this was so beyond gainsaying. Besides, they had a process which could bring about physical alterations in anyone who was presumably of the same fundamental species. They themselves were mammalian; so was Earth's mankind. It would be a relatively simple matter to convert men to their own physical counterparts, thus giving them the greatly added skill of their extraordinary facile appendages. A transplanting of certain cell tissues, a shrinking process equally effective with bone as with flesh. Indeed, man could benefit by retaining his own arms and simply growing six more.'

Creigh had more to say, but I was growing impatient. If I were to set his story down, I'd have to have a little time at the office. What happened to him was not quite clear even to himself. He had scoffed at the suggestion that they could alter the fundamental structure of mankind, and they had been offended. So they had terminated their first interview, but there had been other interviews. More than that—they had fed him their strange food, they had put him under anaesthesia and examined him. By some medicine of their own, they had cured a suppurating ulcer of some years' standing in the space of twenty-four hours. They had given him some kind of ray treatment which had heightened his resistance to disease. They had evidently intended to be friendly. But in the end Creigh must have disappointed them, for they took him back and put him down in approximately the spot from which they had taken off in the first place. He had felt wonderfully exhilarated at first and had got home in double quick time, like a man filled with boundless energy. Afterward that energy began to wear off, quite rapidly; a malaise had set in. And then certain other disturbing things had happened.

'I won't trouble you with an account of those things, Mr Martin. What happened doesn't reflect on those alien creatures from outer space. They meant well. But their knowledge was limited in regard to what the human system could stand, in comparison with their own. You see, Mr Martin, one of the things I learned about them was that they were, by human standards, almost immortal. Not one of them in the laboratory was less than six hundred years old. And their number had been limited by a ruthless weeding out of the weak by a natural process.

'I don't know that it does any good to tell you all this, Mr Martin. No one would believe it if you printed it. It's science fiction, isn't it? That's a name for it.'

With that, he rang the bell, and his daughter appeared as if she had been waiting at the threshold. Undoubtedly she had.

'This way, please, Mr Martin,' she said.

'Thank you, Mr Creigh.'

'Oh, you're welcome. Give my regards to Massingham.'

'If only you'd managed to bring back some sort of proof, Mr Creigh, something to show us — some of their metal, something from the saucer — that sort of thing.'

'The scientific observer demands proof. The nonscientific laymen requires it with even more insistence. I find that ironic, in a way. And amusing. I could offer you proof, Mr Martin. But no one would believe that, either.'

'Listen,' I said. 'You said they were maroon in colour. I thought, in the light before, that your skin. . . .'

He chuckled out of the darkness. He reached out and touched my hand with his, shook it. But something else brushed my hand at almost the same time — a spidery, claw-like touch that made me feel as if I had hit on an electrical outlet.

'I'm waiting, Mr Martin,' said his daughter.

'Be patient, Cissie,' said his voice out of the darkness. 'Goodbye, Mr Martin. If your story is printed, I hope to be able to see it. But I may not live that long; I don't expect to.'

On that note I took my leave. Cissie Creigh remained as cold and impersonal as a robot. It gave me an uncomfortable feeling, and all the way back to the office I couldn't shake off a conviction that what Professor Creigh hadn't told me was considerably more important than what he had.

Tralor looked at what I wrote.

'The damnedest stuff,' he said. 'That boy ought to be writing fiction for the thriller market. What an imagination!'

'Do we run it?'

'Sure,' he said. 'Here's a picture of him. Have a two-column cut made.'

The photograph was that of a somewhat younger man, tall and quite handsome. It was difficult to recognize the man in the darkened room in this photograph. It was an office shot, made for the files at the university, and on the back of it had been set down some of the pertinent data which mortuaries, the military, and college files consider so important. 'Height: six feet. Weight: 185 lbs. Eyes: brown. Race: Caucasian.' And so forth.

The story ran, together with Creigh's picture.

There were heads like this: *Personal Narrative of the Man Who Rode the Saucer! Alien Hordes Invade Earth! To Colonize Earth, Say Saucer People!* The story was done straight, without smart aleck writing, without tongue in cheek. It had the expected results. A few scientists were inclined to take it seriously, depending on independent investigation to verify the site, but on the whole the Creigh account was treated like a second Velikovsky theory. The president of the university personally telephoned to make it clear that Creigh's connection with that institute of higher learning had been severed some time past.

But, of course, investigations turned up nothing.

Before any reports were in, however, something else took place. Ten days after the story's publication, Tralor sent a marked tearsheet to my desk. It was that day's obituary column. He had marked one paragraph, the conventional paragraph:

'Creigh, Henry M., 77 West Malden Street. Last night, after three weeks' illness. . . .'

I went to the funeral, for all that it was set off as private. I sent flowers ahead to thaw out Cissie a little. She had indicated that the funeral was private, and she meant to keep it that way. I got to the house just as they were carrying the casket out. I followed the cortege, which was a very small one, all the way to the cemetery, and there I was barred from admittance. It was by her order, I found out later; all those who had been admitted had carried special cards. I had none.

But what I saw was enough to send me back to the house. I was there waiting for her when Cissie Creigh came back. She was alone.

'Mr Martin,' she said coolly.

'I want to know something, Miss Creigh,' I said.

'I'm sorry. I have nothing to tell you.'

'I think you have. You were the only one with your father. I can't turn up a doctor, unless I look for whoever it was signed the death certificate. So you can tell me.'

'What do you want to know, Mr Martin?'

'What killed your father?'

'I rather think it was the exposure and excitement of his trip.'

'What did the doctor say?'

'He called it advanced deterioration of the major tissues and organs of the body.'

'But what did he name it?'

'He didn't have a name for it.'

'Miss Creigh, honestly, did you believe your father's story?'

'Mr Martin, honestly,' she fenced, 'did you?'

'You're putting me on the spot.'

'So are you me.'

'Let's try again,' I said.

'Let's not,' she answered.

She meant it.

I had a few more seconds. I could have asked the questions I really wanted to ask. But I didn't. I was afraid to ask for fear that she would have answered.

I wanted to know what kind of illness a six-foot man could have had which would have reduced his proportions sufficiently for him to fit into a child's coffin which couldn't have held a human being more than three feet in height at best. I wanted to ask if her father's skin had turned maroon in colour. I wanted to ask whether she knew what her father had meant by his enigmatic statement that the knowledge of those strange saucer people had been limited in regard to what the human system could stand. And most of all I wanted to ask if, by some accident, that coffin had come open, would Henry Creigh have had two arms — or eight?

The True Worth of Ruth Villiers

Michael G. Coney

There were only a few sightseers at this hour, just a dejected handful of gazing ghouls gathered around the fencedoff rectangle of rough scree. A light, drizzling rain sieved through the twilight, fine but penetrating, sufficient to dampen the enthusiasm of the most avid tourist. A camera clicked from time to time, etching on silver bromide the abandoned pit, sunk like a quarry into the hillside and featureless apart from the wooden hut built on top of the shaft. I stood as they stood, elbows resting upon the new fence although, unlike them, I alone had the right to cross the enclosure and enter the hut, if I so wished.

I did not do this. I stayed outside, as though a sightseer. To violate the privacy of the enclosure, to climb down into the pit and enter the shed would have identified me. The watchers would have regarded me, questioning, as I descended, and one of them would have recognized my face from the newspaper photographs of the last few months.

Then they would blame me, condemn me as the man who had left Ruth Villiers to die. They would watch me climbing back up, and I would see it in their faces. Murderer, their expressions would say.

Yet Ruth Villiers still lived, about fifteen feet beneath that wooden shed. . . .

Some six months ago I was sitting in my office, a reasonably contented man with nothing untoward on my mind. If I remember rightly, my attention that day was engaged by a minor problem concerning the upgrading of a local plumber. Such problems form the basis of my job. They can be solved by using a minimum of commonsense allied to a few years experience. Six months ago I considered my work undemanding, but six months ago I had not met Ruth Villiers. Now, I have still not met the girl face to face, and I wish to God I could. . . .

The plumber sat opposite me, cap twisting in his hands involuntarily, as though he were divining water, clad spottily in his working clothes.

'My income for the past year, Mr—er——' he glanced at the nameplate on my desk '—Archer, was one thousand three hundred and seventy Creds. My present Social Value Cred Rating is two thousand three hundred Creds.' He looked aggrieved. They always do. It is part of the stock in trade of my customers, this hangdog look as though they alone are condemned to poverty in a world of affluence.

'You consider that you should be upgraded?' I asked. I knew what he considered, of course, but I enjoyed watching people sweat it out, six months ago.

'Yes,' he replied with timid aggression, like a cornered sheep.

I slid his file towards me and opened it, making play of adjusting my bifocals. He was right about his income, at any rate. It was there in black and white Cr. 1,370, as returned to the Inland Revenue.

Taking my ball-point, I computed the familiar sum:

Earnings entitlement—equals 1½ times gross		
annual income Equals 1½ times 1,370	Cr.	1,955
Plus Basic Individual Entitlement		
(Commonly known as 'Birthright')	Cr.	600
Total	Cr.	2,555

Obviously the nervous little plumber had a case. He was due to be elevated two steps, to a Social Value Cred Rating of Cr. 2,500. He must have worked his guts out last year, poor devil, and now he wanted to reap some sort of reward, status-wise.

'I'll look into it,' I promised. 'We'll let you know. Next!' I pressed a button on the desk ostentatiously, cutting short any possible argument. He walked out backwards as though I were royalty. Instead of the next customer, my clerk Eccles entered, breathless.

'Emergency, Mr Archer!' he panted. We had emergencies every day, actually, but he never got used to them. He still twittered with panic at the first sign of a claim computation, which was why he was still my clerk, instead of managing a District of his own.

'Send him in,' I said calmly, expecting to see some bereaved pensioner who wanted an advance to bury his wife. I frequently get sorrowful relatives touting for handouts, but sorrow is relative—to quote a private joke between Eccles and me—and each case is treated strictly on merit. Tears of sorrow will not blind a person to the possibility of a benefit and we generally find that the wetter the cheeks, the more outrageously the Department will be soaked.

'Er . . . it's not a death case, Mr Archer.' Eccles corrected me. 'It's a real emergency. An accident claim. There's no next of kin, either. Just this lad, says his name's Jack Griffiths. Boy-friend of claimant.'

'Oh.' I thought for a moment. 'Well, you'd better send him in, just the same.' It was filthy luck getting an accident claim today, when Forbes was expected at any hour.

Forbes, I must explain, is our Regional Director. His job, which I imagine he enjoys, is to travel about the various Districts within his Region, raising Cain. His favourite pastime is going through the case files with a magnifying glass, trying to establish that I have wasted public funds through being oversympathetic.

Perhaps I ought to amplify at this point, as not everyone is familiar with the workings of the Department of Social Value. It goes like this.

Suppose someone is in hospital, awaiting an expensive operation. The obvious question poses itself: is the patient worth treating, bearing in mind his value to the community? So the hospital sends me a claim based on the estimated cost.

Then I call the National Bank and find that the patient has accumulated savings totalling (say) Cr. 2,000 to date.

And I consult my own punch-card index and find that he has a Social Value Cred Rating of (say) Cr. 1,500.

That person, therefore, is worth Cr. 3,500 to the community. Nothing more; nothing less.

So if the operation costs up to Cr. 3,500, the scalpels will flash and he will be healed, presumably.

But if the operation (including pre- and post-operational care and treatment) is estimated at Cr. 3,501, his flesh will remain uncarved. He can, however, receive lesser treatment and drugs to the value of Cr. 3,500, at which point he will be discharged from the hospital. What he does then is up to him; but assuming he is able to start work again he must repay the loan of Cr. 1,500 on his Social Value Cred Rating before he can start to accumulate any personal savings again. In repaying this amount he will be allowed the bare minimum of his wages for living expenses. In fact, he will probably be fed and lodged by his friends, provided they are not caught doing it. Undue Sympathy is a punishable offence, and rightly so, because why should one man secure an unearned advantage over his fellows?

Years ago in the midtwentieth there was a National Health Service whereby all doctors' and hospital bills were paid by the state. There were other Social Services too, in the nature of Unemployment Benefits, Retirement Pensions, etcetera. In other words, people were actively encouraged to spend time in hospital or otherwise out of work, and discouraged from saving for their retirement.

This unfortunate system remained on the backs of the British for over fifty years, until the population crisis of the early 2000s and the emergence of the Darwinist party of which I am the local Branch Secretary. Opponents of our party might say that we stand for the survival of the fittest, but we prefer to think of the Darwinist system as fair shares for each, according to his ability.

It is a beautifully simple system, ideal in our country, where all property belongs to the state, unlike other less progressive nations I could name. Our only personal possessions are the SVC rating and accumulated savings in the National Bank. Savings revert to the state on death.

All the same, you can see what I mean about the temptation which might face a weak Valuation Officer on occasions to be oversympathetic.

Anyway, in came Jack Griffiths, boy-friend of claimant, looking sick.

'What can I do for you, Mr Griffiths?' I asked formally.

'It's not me . . .' he stammered. 'It's my girl-friend, Ruth. Ruth Villiers. There's been an accident. . . .'

'Oh. Well, strictly speaking, I am only empowered to deal with claimants personally, otherwise we could all spend each others' money, couldn't we? So I'm afraid you'll have to take me to her. You must realize that these things have to be done properly.'

'Oh, my God.' He looked stricken, poor little sod. I pictured Ruth Villiers in some remote hospital with both legs broken, unable to receive anything but the most basic attention until the formalities had been gone through. It's on occasions like this when I wonder whether the system couldn't be streamlined a little, giving everyone an emergency allowance of (say) Cr. 200.

'Well, where is she?' I asked again.

He bit his lip, hesitating. 'You can't see her,' he said at last. 'There's been a fall at the old Wheal Pentire mine. . . . I think she's OK but I can't get to her. She would have been up at the face; there's a big chamber there with walls of granite. I can't see that collapsing. . . . But the whole of the entrance is caved in, and she's inside. How can you *see* her, under that lot?'

That was the beginning of the Ruth Villiers affair and like most intricate problems in my business it appeared simple at first hearing. All that was required of me was a trip to the Wheal Pentire mine—an abandoned working near Camborne-Redruth—a quick, expert assessment of the situation, then a yes or no as to the feasibility of digging the trapped girl out. Obviously I would exercise my discretion in treating the boy-friend as next of kin.

Two hours later I stood at the mine entrance with Jack Griffiths, both of us in heavy overcoats with collars turned up against the biting wind which, over the years, had sculpted the stunted trees into streamlined teardrop forms. I often wondered why those old miners chose such desolate situations for their pits, and whenever I see those broken chimneys which punctuate the bleak countryside I can imagine the craggy Cornishmen scratching the grudging earth for tin with masochistic enjoyment.

Wheal Pentire was small as such mines go. The entrance was indicated by the rotting remains of a shed and a rusty narrow-gauge track which ran up to the abrupt hillside and terminated at a heap of tumbled boulders.

'We were larking about,' Griffiths explained tensely, staring fascinated at the rock-face. 'We've often been in there before; right up as far as the old face half-way through the hill. Anyway, Ruth ran in there and I went in after her. I heard her laughing, way ahead of me, just before I ran into the prop . . .'

He went on to describe it; how the pit-prop, rotten with years, had shifted and begun to crumble. A few stones pattering from the roof had become a roaring collapse in a matter of seconds and he had just made it outside. His voice was bitter, and I sensed a degree of self-condemnation. He felt that there was something he should have done, something more than just saving his own skin and going for help. It was useless telling him that his actions had been the only ones possible in the circumstances; he was intent on blaming himself.

Anyway, there was the fall, and somewhere in the middle of the hill was Ruth Villiers, possibly unhurt and approximately two hundred yards from the mine entrance. The cave-in looked extensive; I could see a depression in the rising shale of the barren hillside, running for some distance and marking the course of the collapse until it merged with the general rise of the broken ground.

Griffiths was regarding me wide-eyed, awaiting the opinion which could mean the life or death of his girl-friend. 'Can you do anything?' he asked at last.

I had already consulted the Social Value Register and found that Ruth had a rating of Cr. 1,200. She was only seventeen and worked as a Grade VI in the South-Western Agricultural Centre, so her income was just Cr. 400 per annum. This gave her an Earnings Entitlement of (1½) Cr. 600, plus Basic Individual Entitlement of Cr. 600.

Cr. 1,200. It could be done, just.

'I'll have to get a surveyor in,' I told Griffiths. 'But it seems to me that if we brought in a GEX 2/6 R excavator and took out a pit about there'—I pointed to a spot about fifty yards beyond the apparent limit of the cave-in—'we could break into the tunnel from the side, without bringing down any more of the roof. . . . Assuming she's safe, is there plenty of air?'

'I think so. The tunnel opens out into quite a big chamber near the face.'

'She'll have to go hungry for a while. We won't be able to sink a preliminary shaft, not on Cr. 1,200. Has she got any savings?'

'Oh, yes,' he said eagerly. 'We were saving up to get married. She's got a balance of about Cr. 300 at the National Bank.'

'Good. That's Cr. 1,500 altogether. I think we should be able to manage on that,' I said, feeling like God. 'We'll go back, now, and I'll work out the figures.'

'How soon before we get her out?' he asked anxiously, staring at the hillside.

'About three days, I should think,' I replied confidently. 'She'll be hungry, but that's the least of our worries.'

Symptomatic of our times? Yes. The thought of a terrified girl trapped underground for three days worried me not one bit. After all, I didn't know her; to me she was just a number on the Register. So the number was temporarily missing underground? Never mind; there was every chance of it reappearing again, thus balancing the books. Griffiths looked at me strangely, but then he was not a valuation officer. I deal with cases like this all the time.

Back at the office, I settled down with the manual of plant rates. I find this type of work very interesting; it's one of the few instances when there is scope for initiative in my job.

Anyway, the initial figures were soon out and I had an unpleasant surprise. They were way over the top:

Ruth Villiers—estimated cost sheet

Surveyor's fees	75
Hire of GEX 2/6 R at Cr. 13 per hour. 72 hours (say)	936
Wages of operators—3 shifts including night bonus and travelling time	200
Transport of GEX 2/6 R to and from site	260
Accommodation and food of operators	10
Floodlights and electricity for night working	20
Incidentals	50
	1,551

Griffiths' face was dull with shock when I showed him the cost sheet. 'I thought you said it could be done,' he muttered, accusing. 'I thought you said Cr. 1,500 would be enough.' He ran down the sheet with a slender finger which shook a little. 'Incidentals Cr. 50?' he queried. 'What's that, for Christ's sake? Your rake-off?'

I fought to contain a rising tide of annoyance. 'My services are provided free by the State,' I informed him shortly. 'Incidentals cover a number of things and Cr. 50 may be a conservative estimate. Basically, you need that sort of money to pay the men extra above the standard rate, so they'll get on with the job. There are other expenses, of course; but that's the main item. Gratuities.'

'What!' Griffiths was white-faced. 'Are you saying that you have to tip the buggers to work hard, when there's a girl's life at stake?'

'Well, yes . . . . Look here, Griffiths,' I said kindly, 'you've got to see it their way. They don't know your girl from Eve. To them, she's just another job, and when that job's done, well, they might be on idle pay. So they tend to spin it out a bit. It's cheaper to give them an unofficial bonus and charge it to incidentals than it would be to have to hire the excavator for another day.'

'Christ.' Griffiths was shivering; he sat opposite me across the desk, looking lost. This sort of thing was new to him; he had no experience of the careful negotiations inherent in labour relations.

He was looking so wretched, in fact, that I began to feel genuinely sorry for him. 'There's still a chance,' I said gently, 'if you're prepared to take it.'

'What's that?'

'We do without the surveyor. We just hire the men and the excavator, and start to dig. I've got a plan here'—I pulled out a yellowed sheet of paper—'of the old workings. I think we can take a chance on it and dig here.' I had already marked the possible starting place. 'In fact, we've got to take this chance. It's the only one you've got. This way, the maximum cost should be about Cr. 1,476. Provided we don't strike any snags, we should be OK.'

'Cutting it fine, even then,' Griffiths was nibbling his fingernails.

'I realize that.' I folded up the plan, 'Can I take it you agree? There's a lot to get organized.'

' OK.' He got to his feet.

'See you at the site tomorrow,' I said.

He showed me a photograph of her, of the two of them together, taken while they were on holiday three months previously. Ruth Villiers was an insignificant-looking girl; mousey hair, pale complexion, weak features. It was a full-length shot and my chief impression was that she looked the sort of girl who might have trouble in childbirth. You see this type of woman a lot, these days; despite Darwinism and encouragement for the fittest. It's as though Nature, jealous of the success of humanity in other directions, is trying to foul things up biologically.

I didn't say anything, though. Griffiths looked at the photograph for a long time before replacing it in his battered wallet. We both stood silent for a while, stamping our feet and waiting for the excavator to arrive.

It was a misty morning of late autumn and the scene looked particularly desolate; the crumbling, barren shale hillside, the stunted trees almost bereft of leaves, the rusty, overgrown rails disappearing under the menacing mountain of rubble. The sky merged into the damp hills and the air was harsh and moist.

The place had a weird atmosphere; you could imagine, vividly, the old miners coughing their tubercular way to the face, grimy hands gripping sodden packets of cornish pasties. It's said that they used to make the pasties of pilchards, wrapping the fish in a bone-hard casing of pastry of such durability that the food could be dropped down a fifty-foot shaft without shattering. Nowadays they make pasties for the tourists, of minced algaemeat clad in starchate, and I daresay the taste is no worse.

A rumbling from the valley announced the arrival of the excavator; soon we could see it, a huge yellow-tracked vehicle winding its laborious way along the misty lane, on the back of a low-loader, swaying top-heavy. The truck pulled up and the driver descended from the cab to join us, flicking his cigarette to the ground in a damp sizzle.

'Where do you want it?' he asked tersely.

I pointed up the hillside and he pursed his lips. 'Tricky, that,' he said. 'They overbalance easily, do these excavators. I'm not sure Jeff can take her up there. No. I don't like the look of that at all.'

A van pulled up and a succession of men climbed out, stretching their limbs.

'Jeff!' Our companion called across.

''Ullo.' A large, pot-bellied man in blue overalls lumbered towards us.

'Gent says you've got to take it up there.'

'Oh?' Jeff scratched his head. 'Well, I don't like the looks of that. Tricky stuff, shale. Start sliding on that lot and she'll be over before you can say knife. Don't stand a chance, if that happens. If she rolls, the cab crushes like a matchbox.'

Resignedly I reached in my pocket and drew out Ruth Villiers' National Bank card and punch. Jeff produced his own card with alacrity. I punched Cr. 2 on his receipts side and he punched a similar amount on Ruth's payments side.

The first incidental had been incurred.

Griffiths was watching; as soon as the men had shambled back to the excavator he spoke.

'What's to stop me paying Cr. 500 into her account, to be on the safe side?' He asked, like so many before him. They must take us for fools.

Once again I explained. 'As soon as the Claim is notified, the account is frozen. The only item which can be credited to a frozen account is arrears of wages genuinely earned to a maximum of one week. Just that one item, nothing more, Otherwise the system would be meaningless, don't you see? Any relative could pay money into the claimant's account and say it was the repayment of an old loan, or something.'

'I suppose so,' said Griffiths heavily.

'I could tell you some stories.' I went on, warming to my pet subject. 'It's amazing the way some people try to get round the law. I had a case once —— '

'Look,' interrupted Griffiths suddenly. His fists were clenched white. 'I'm not interested in any of your bloody stories! What's more, I'm sick of the way you seem to treat this whole business as an academic exercise. Don't you realize there's a girl under there? A human being, like you and me? She's trapped under there, and all you can think of is the interesting technical ramifications! For God's sake, haven't you any pity?' He was obviously overwrought.

'Take it easy,' I laid a hand on his shoulder. 'I realize it's your girl down there, and I'm sorry. I had a claimant die in hospital yesterday, and I'm sorry about that too. Since the Social Valuation Act came in, over nine thousand people have died who, before 2012, might have been saved. I'm sorry about them. But it's for the general good. Starving Chineses are dying like flies and I'm sorry for them. But perhaps that's for the general good, too. Now, how sorry can you get? You've got to learn to accept these things.'

'I suppose so,' muttered Griffiths after a pause. He didn't agree with me, really. He just didn't want to antagonize the one person who might be able to help.

A black saloon drew up behind the workmen's van and a neatly-dressed man got out. He picked his way through the loose shale towards us.

'Press,' he announced concisely, producing a card. 'I understand there's a young girl trapped under there.'

'That's right,' Griffiths said eagerly. I could see what he was thinking. This man might, through his paper, wield some influence. Perhaps he could drum up public sympathy, causing such an outcry that some sort of official grant would be forthcoming. Griffiths went on to describe the situation but I could have told him he was wasting his time. Once you made one grant, everybody would be queueing up, and the system would collapse.

'Thanks,' said the man from the *National Daily* eventually, folding his notebook and slipping it smoothly into his pocket. 'Now. Do you mind if I take a photograph?' He was a very polite reporter. He took a photograph of Griffiths looking sick, the background a pile of rubble.

'Good,' he said. 'Now what about the young girl, Ruth? You don't happen to have a snapshot of her I could use, I suppose?'

'Certainly.' Griffiths produced his photo, handing it over.

The newspaperman examined it closely, tilting it at different angles, covering parts of it with his hand, whistling tunelessly under his breath. 'Yes,' he said at last, handing it back. 'Yes. I'll let you know if I need it. Actually, I'm not sure if I shall be able to use this story at all. It lacks. . . er. . . interest. No meat in it. Quite possibly a wasted journey, I'm afraid . . . Ah, well.' He shuffled his feet, extended his hand to each of us in turn. 'I'd better be getting back.' He left.

'What was all that about?' asked Griffiths, vaguely annoyed by the man's abrupt departure.

'You heard what he said. He's not interested. I don't think it matters. A newspaper story would have made things worse, bringing sightseers along, getting in the way.'

His reply was drowned by a sudden roar from the excavator. It moved forward, tilted, and ran off the low-loader to the stony ground. Turning, tracks screaming, it churned away up the shale slope, Jeff gazing down at us from the high cab.

Work had commenced.

I departed at about five o'clock that afternoon, leaving Griffiths standing in the drizzling rain watching the men rig the arc-lights. I went straight home. I didn't feel up to calling at the office; in short, I was dead beat. There was something about the situation—the callousness of the workmen at the site, the motives of the reporter, the general attitude of everyone including myself which had stirred me up during the day, twisting my guts until I was hating them all, me most of all. I couldn't forget that plain little teenager buried under the hillside.

It was bad, this sensation which could only be described as sympathy, and I tried to expunge it from my mind. It could lose me my job, turn me into one of the faceless thousands I see every morning riding the conveyor to the South-Western Industrial Centre. I could become like Griffiths, a machine operator on Cr. 800 p.a. Doris wouldn't like that; she was very conscious of social rating. I remember an occasion when we had to ride the conveyor during the rush hour, due to minor trouble with the car. I can see Doris's face now, that frozen look as she stood swaying to the motion, surrounded by the workers in their overalls. She was withdrawn, mentally huddled within herself as though by so doing she could minimize the effect of physical contact with the masses. I may appear to be standing with them, she seemed to be saying, but spiritually I am elsewhere, way above them.

And quite true, when her husband, me, brings home Cr. 4,000 per annum. Her spirit can afford to live it up. All men are created equal, they say, and they prove it by the Basic Individual Entitlement of Cr. 600. But then, as time passes, Nature takes its course and the pushers get to the top. Like me. Whereas Griffiths and his ugly little girl-friend stay behind, unable to rise from the viscous masses. And why not? Because they are no longer equal. They have proved themselves inferior. This is Darwinism.

It's a good system. The only fair system.

So that night I went out and got drunk and when I got back I was sick, and Doris became unpleasant about it. I told her to go to hell; loudly, so that the neighbours would hear. The people in the next apartment have a Social Credit Rating of a mere Cr. 1,500; God knows how they can afford the place.

All next day I sat in my office wondering how things were going at the site. No sign of Forbes, and just as well. I could do without the tension occasioned by a full-scale examination of the books.

The day after, about one o'clock, I could stand it no longer. I told Eccles I was going out; and went, before he could start twittering about all the appointments he had arranged for that afternoon. I took the car to the site.

As I climbed out of the car—it was not raining, thank heavens—I could see the lone figure of Griffiths standing disconsolate on the hillside, a huge chunk of which had been bitten out by the tyrannosaurus jaws of the excavator. He was gazing into the pit, the bottom of which I could not see from my present position. The scene was curiously silent, the excavator motionless. It appeared that operations had temporarily halted and I imagined the workmen had deemed it time to claim further incidental expenses. I made my way up the slope.

'What's going on?' I asked Griffiths.

His expression was blank; he looked at me blindly, unfocused, then his gaze returned to the pit.

The men were leaning against the grounded jaws of the excavator, smoking. They looked up as I scrambled down towards them.

'You've got troubles,' one of them said flatly, the cigarette at his lip twitching in time to the words.

'Oh, for Christ's sake . . . . I looked around seeking some explanation of their inactivity, and failing. They were waiting for me to ask them. 'What's the difficulty?' I asked.

Not replying, the man Jeff took up a crowbar and tapped the ground graphically, with a ringing sound. I bent down and brushed the loose shale aside with my palm.

They had struck a stratum of solid granite.

Avoiding the stricken look from Griffiths as I climbed back out of the pit, I made my way down the hillside to the car.

Seating myself, I tried to think constructively, but all I could accomplish was self-condemnation. This was my fault. True, I couldn't have known that the granite was there; but it was I who had dispensed with the advice of a surveyor on the grounds of expense. I had made a mistake, one which had probably cost Ruth Villiers her life—always assuming she was alive at present. And she quite possibly was alive, perfectly safe in that granite chamber which Griffiths had originally told me about and which I, in my anxiety to cut costs, had forgotten.

I sat there for a while. I could see the others, Griffiths now joined by the workmen, standing on the edge of the pit and gazing down the hill at me, waiting for a decision as to the next step . . . .

OK. So I would make the decision. The frustrations of the past few days had built up to a knot of fire in my stomach; I suddenly found that I was shaking. I flung open the car door.

There was a field telephone at the pit connected by a temporary cable to the excavation gang's headquarters in the village. I would use that to order, on my own authority, a mechanical rock-breaker and team. I would stall the Credit Requisition when it passed through my office and, by the time the delay was discovered, Ruth Villiers would be free.

Then I would face the music and the loss of my job, and the abrupt fall in my Social Credit Rating as they forced me to repay the credit I had, in effect, stolen. For everything must be in balance, that is the System . . . .

Well, sod the System.

I was half-walking, half-running back up the hill when a shout from behind caused me to stop and look back. Another car had drawn up, the driver was waving to me urgently. The passenger door opened.

Forbes stepped out.

He climbed towards me briskly, bowlerhatted, bespectacled, thin face lined with many years of seeking out discrepancies.

'I hear you've been having some difficulty up here,' he said, looking at me keenly and sizing up in practiced fashion my distraught appearance. He had seen this sort of thing before. 'You weren't thinking of doing anything foolish, were you? No ... No ...' He smiled thinly. 'Of course you weren't. You're a careful man, Archer. A man after my own heart. Now. What seems to be the trouble?'

'As I see it, the position is this.'

Forbes was talking in that verbose civil-servanty way he has—I wonder if I talk like that?—and we were all grouped round listening while he indicated his computations with a delicately-held ballpoint.

'Miss Villiers, provided she is still alive, has Cr. 400 left to her name, which is obviously insufficient for financing an endeavour to break through this granite. Hire of mobile breaker for one day, with crew, Cr. 500.' He tapped the figures again. 'And it is not permitted to hire such expensive equipment for a period of less than a day, even if you could get through in that time.'

'So?' I asked, deferential. How much did Forbes really suspect? Could he possibly know that I came near to exhibiting Undue Sympathy?

'There is one course open to us now, and one only.' He spoke gravely, looking at Griffiths.

'Yes?' Griffiths was eager for some hope, any hope.

'We must utilize the remaining Cr. 400 in the best possible way, which is firstly to sink a shaft through to the chamber for air and food. This, I estimate, will cost all of Cr. 200 even with the high-speed mobile drill I propose using. Which leaves Cr. 200. For food.'

He stopped talking and no one else started. We were all, I think, working it out. Ruth Villiers was unable to earn money while she was down there. So when the Cr. 200 was finished, so was she.

Griffiths spoke at last, huskily. 'But Cr. 200 . . . that's food for about . . . seven or eight months. So what you mean is, she just stays down there, buried alive until her food runs out! For God's sake, you can't mean that! Where's your humanity?' He clutched Forbes' sleeve.

Forbes stood still for a while and I felt that this was, for once, a job which he was not enjoying.

Then he disengaged himself from Griffiths' grasp. 'Well,' he replied calmly, 'that's the System. It's not humanity's fault that your girl got herself trapped down there, is it?' He paused, and I like to think that his next words were meant in all sincerity.

'If I were you, I would pray that she strikes gold.'

He walked away, and soon his car was moving off down the lane to the village.

'Christ . . . .' Griffiths was gazing after the receding vehicle. 'So that's the sort of man that runs things. Mr Archer,' his voice shook, 'isn't there anything we can do? Isn't there any hope at all?' His eyes kept drifting away, up the hill where the excavator stood motionless. 'Can't you tell the men to carry on?'

'There's no point,' I replied quietly. 'They'll never get through with that machine, not if they tried for a month.'

'It's not right!' he burst out. 'Not for the sake of a few lousy Credits. What good is that to anyone? You could spare the money, so could I, if we were allowed to. The System is all wrong!'

'The System's OK,' I said. 'It's just that, now and then, we get situations arise where our judgment is clouded by personal involvement. Look at those men up there.' I gestured towards the workmen packing their tools and preparing the excavator for departure. 'They don't care, because they don't know your girl-friend.'

'But surely it's not *right* that they don't care?'

'Let's forget that. Look at it this way. The economists have worked out exactly how much this country is worth, and have estimated its future worth with reasonable accuracy. Now the country consists of people, and it's only right that the people should have a fair share in all this wealth. Right?'

'I suppose so.'

'And when I say a fair share, I mean just that. Every person gets no more, no less than his entitlement. Now supposing you had five people dying in hospital because each of them needed twenty Credits more for an operation. Would you split an unforeseen Cr. 100 up between them, and save all five, or would you use it to rescue Ruth?'

'Your way, they all die. Six altogether.' Griffiths spoke bitterly. I wasn't getting through to him.

'Yes, but look at it from the point of view of the country as a whole,' I continued determinedly. 'Once, years ago, we used to have a problem. Only the rich could afford heart transplants, and the rich were usually old, or they wouldn't need the operation. So they were able to spend Cr. 10,000 on an operation which prolonged their life say five years. That money would have paid for fifty kidney transplants and saved the lives of fifty young, useful people.

'This can't happen now, because nobody can get that rich, not since the Abolition of Personal Property Act of 2009. So now, nobody gets heart transplants. But very few die of diseased kidneys. Now wouldn't you say that the people, as a whole, have benefited from this?'

Griffiths seemed calmer now. 'What you have told me is quite logical,' he said slowly. 'There's just one thing, though . . . .'

'What's that?'

'Why don't *you* like the System?'

'But I do. I still say the System is the finest in the world.'

And I was still saying it to myself six hours later, doggedly, as the mobile probe withdrew its drill and the voice of Ruth Villiers drifted up to us from the depths.

Yes, that was six months ago almost to the day. The story appeared in the *National Daily*, of course; it was too good to miss. The girl was different, however. The sad-eyed waif with beautiful, regular features who twisted the nation's heart-strings from the pages of the paper was a far cry from Griffiths' lumpy girl-friend.

That's what brought the sightseers, of course. Even now, after all this time, those dismal, raincoated figures around the fence were imagining the girl of the press photograph . down there, and thinking what a shame it was that a lovely girl like that should be wasted. And how they would like to rescue her, Lancelot-like, and take her away from the dreary pit, telling her it would be all right now and, soothing her with words and actions, carry her off to bed . . . .

I wanted to shout at them, to shake them by the shoulders and yell into their avid faces: She's ugly! She's got a wart on the side of her nose and she stinks because she hasn't washed for six months! You understand that? Now! Does it make any *difference?*

Griffiths was emerging from the shed; he'd been bringing her liquid food twice a day, spending all his spare time talking to her down the narrow, polythene-lined shaft.

He didn't speak much to me, now. He had become furtive, and would rarely tell me what they talked about over the hours. I don't know why I wanted to know: I think I had an almighty guilt complex about the whole affair and wished to share in it as much as possible, as though by so doing I might dilute the individual grief . . . .

Griffiths was hurrying towards me, scrambling up the pit side, fingers scrabbling in the shale. Something was wrong.

'Mr Archer!'

I vaulted the fence and slid down towards him, skinning my hands on the loose rock in my haste. We met abruptly on the steep slope and clung together, breathless and tottering.

'What's the trouble?' I gasped.

'She won't speak. She's been bad, today, and now she won't speak to me. I heard her, she made a queer noise, but she wouldn't say anything!' His eyes were dilated with fear.

Seconds later I was standing in the gloom of the shed, calling down the tube which served Ruth Villiers for ventilation, communication and supplies.

'Ruth!'

I put my ear to the tube, listening hard. I could hear faint scuffling noises as though she was shifting about; but she didn't speak.

'Ruth!' I called again. 'Are you all right?'

There was a sudden, complete silence from below. Griffiths was bending close to me, face averted and strained, trying himself to catch some faint sound from the tube. The interior of the shed smelled damp and musty, and on the table beside the stand which supported the tube was a half-empty milk bottle. The top quarter-inch of the milk had turned a viscous yellow and particles of sour solid adhered to the inside of the neck. A cup stood on the table also, stained in ochre ring below the rim and containing a brown puddle of old, cold tea.

Clear and distinct from the tube came the unmistakable cry of a new-born baby.

I've called for the breaking team and they should be here within the hour. I hope to have Ruth Villiers and the baby above ground in about six hours, so nobody can say that the Department doesn't move fast, when occasion demands.

Griffiths is beside himself with delight, crooning down the tube to his new daughter, planning the future—not forgetting the wedding—with Ruth. I wonder whether he knew of her condition, all along? Or whether she never told him, for fear that he would shirk any responsibility and clear out, leaving her completely alone? I don't know. There are depths to Griffiths that I will never be able to sound. But one thing I do know—and I can see it in his face now, as he talks down the tube—here is a man utterly in love, and with a girl at whom I myself would not look twice. It takes all sorts.

And just as well, too. The System may proclaim for the sake of economics that we are all basically equal but with individual capabilities of varying social value, but I wonder whether there aren't things—emotions, relationships, even love—which are incapable of being measured in terms of Credits.

Don't take me for a revolutionary. The last few hours

have shown the System in an extremely good light, which I trust the *National Daily* will not be slow to publicise. My own faith, which I admit was shaken at one time, has been restored by the wonderfully logical way in which the System coped with the final sequence of events.

Because in that moment of birth in the underground cavern, one person became two: Ruth Villiers, with her virtually exhausted Social Credit Rating. . . .

And her daughter, with a Basic Individual Entitlement—Birthright—of Cr. 600. More than enough to hire a team of breakers.

Surely, now, nobody can criticize the System. Not even the *National Daily*.

Not even me.

Quest

Lee Harding

Behind the desk sat the Divisional Controller. Tall, gaunt, expressionless, the skin stretched tightly across the unyielding bones of his face, his lips moving with mechanical precision.

'And what exactly is it that you want, Mr Johnston?'

Before him, on the other side of the wide desk, sat a small, pale, insignificant little man with his hands tied nervously together. His eyes were troubled, his manner uneasy.

'Something *real*,' he said. 'Something that hasn't been made by man. Something that isn't synthetic. That's all. Not to keep. Only to see. So that I will at least know that it is there. Where can I find such a thing?'

The Controller looked perplexed. It was the first time he had come across such a request. 'Something...*real*?' His lips formed the word as if it was alien to his vocabulary. 'What are the grounds for your request, Mr Johnston?'

The little man's hopes dwindled. How could he possibly explain this inexplicable desire that had swollen into an obsession, in words capable of being comprehended by the sombre individual seated opposite him?'

Behind the Controller a wide window gaped at the world. Mr Johnston saw the city stretching away from him like the carapace of some gigantic crustacean. He stared bleakly at the towering confections of steel and plastic contesting dominance of the horizon, and shuddered.

'All around me I see a world made by man,' he began, hesitantly. 'The city we live in, the air we breathe, the clothes we wear and even the food we eat are products of our marvellous technology. Everywhere I see evidence of mankind's incredible skill—but where do I find the heart? And how can I find my own when there is only this grim, awful world of gaunt buildings and unsmiling people to relate my feelings to? Surely, there must be some tiny place that has not been swallowed by the relentless maw of human progress?'

He gave a restless sigh, and slumped back in his chair. 'It wasn't always like this. Even I know that. I must have been born in the twilight of the old world and the beginning of the new. I can remember trees and flowers and the sounds of birds. Wide streams of water passing by my feet. And clouds and rains and cold winds. Today I ask myself—what is a bird? What is a cloud? Is there no longer room for them on this earth we have *made*? Have they gone for ever, never to return? Have our machines finally glutted themselves on the great banquet of our planet and left nothing but a barren core sheathed in metal, wandering aimlessly through space with no winter or summer to mark its passage?'

Emotion, a dark stain newly risen to colour the little man's wan cheeks a fiery crimson, now faded. He stared emptily out through the window at the terrifying landscape.

The Controller was silent. Behind his shrewd, calculating eyes a razor-sharp intellect was busy digesting the information Johnston had spread before him, and was already preparing a carefully studied reply.

'But you haven't told me *why* you feel that you must have this something real.'

Why? Mr Johnston didn't really know. 'I must have it, that's all,' he answered, a note of near desperation in his outburst. 'Something I can touch with my own two hands and know that it is real, that it hasn't been made by man, but by . . . .'

'By *whom*, Mr Johnston?'

The little man looked into the eyes of the Controller. He

imagined that he caught a faint flicker of cynicism in their icy dispassion. He swallowed quickly. 'By . . . by . . .' *By whom?* 'I . . . I don't know, really. Only . . . only that it will not have been made by man. Don't you understand? Something *real.*'

The Controller permitted himself the luxury of a smile. 'But Mr Johnston, surely you realize . . . .'

At that precise moment his inquisitor's facial muscles seemed to suddenly freeze. A blank, rigid expression leapt into the cold eyes and they seemed to be fixed on a point in the air somewhere behind Mr Johnston. From a hidden place somewhere between the Controller's shoulder blades a thin wisp of smoke curled lazily towards the ceiling.

'You must . . . pardon me,' he stammered. 'I fear that a . . . sudden adverse . . . overload has . . . *has* . . .' On the desk in front of him were two hands curled into tight fists of impotence. 'Overwork . . . you understand. Undue . . . stress. I . . . if you would be . . . so kind . . . as to . . . go along to . . . room twelve you will be . . . attended to. I . . . I . . . please forgive this . . . this . . . *this* delay. I . . . .'

He said no more. His mouth froze into a vacant oval. There was a brief scatter of sparks within depths of his eyes. The curl of smoke thickened momentarily and then dispersed.

Johnston stared at the immobile figure for another moment or two. There was a bleak hopeless expression on his face. Then he sighed, and got up and left the room.

Whatever was happening to the world, he wondered. Machines that looked like people and people who looked like machines. Each day it became more difficult to tell one from the other.

He took the elevator to the ground floor and hurried outside. There was no sense in going to Room 12 and having to sit through yet another fruitless interview with yet another humanoid extension of some master computer. And besides, he had begun to realize that the concept of something real was beyond the programming of the city cybers.

And not only the machines, he thought, as he turned to watch the people moving silently around him. Their blank, purposeless manner seemed more appropriate to a machine than a creature of flesh and blood. There was something in their blank incomprehension when he asked them about his problem that had frightened him, and sent him to his Divisional Controller for assistance.

It had been rather a nasty shock to discover that his friendly inquisitor was a robot. Under the circumstances he should have expected it, for there were not many jobs of administration these days that were not entrusted to the widely dispersed cyber units. Robotics had become so incredibly complex that Johnston wouldn't have been at all surprised to find out that more than half the city's population was robotic, no matter how cleverly they were disguised.

He started walking. In no particular direction. Overhead wan sunlight from a bald sky drove a wedge between the towering ramparts of the city and sought the pavements below.

Johnston looked up at the dizzying cliffs of steel rising around him and marvelled at the way they clambered drunkenly towards the sky. Incredible blocks of artificiality marching doggedly towards infinity.

Was there really an end to this city?

He had travelled all the surface and subterranean commuters in the hope of finding the perimeters where the monstrous canyons called streets gave way to more level circumstances, and where he might begin to feel the weight of sunlight upon his body.

He must have travelled miles in every direction, but always the city remained unchanged, and the farthest he could travel was to arrive back at his point of departure.

So had Johnston's nightmare begun. This terrible vision of a world encompassed by a solitary city that stretched from east to west and from pole to pole, covering the old world with the fused magma of man's work.

Was that the legacy of the Gods?

He didn't want to believe that. He *couldn't* believe that the past had been obliterated. Something must remain. If only he could find it.

Perhaps it would give him courage to face his bleak tomorrows.

Had he really explored all the avenues? What other means of transport were there? Air-cars, elevators.

Elevators!

But of course! There were more dimensions than one. He had searched *around* him, but he had never looked either down or up.

Excited, he made directly for one of the largest Administration buildings.

The elevator door slid open as he approached.

'Where to?' asked an impersonal voice from nowhere.

'Down,' said Mr Johnston.

'How far?'

'As far as I can go.'

The machine clucked to itself. The door slid shut. Then Johnston was being whisked into the bowels of the earth.

The lift fell at an incredible speed. He could sense that mile after mile of city was collecting above him and yet there was no sensation of moving. The lift was carefully balanced on a shaft of null-grav. He felt as light as the air within the cube.

The elevator finally came to a rest. The door slid back and Johnston stepped out.

And was dismayed. Before him stretched a long, empty corridor. A uniformed figure stood waiting.

'Sir,' he said. 'Your name?'

'Johnston, Harry Johnston. I . . . I was just having a look around.'

'Ah, I see. I will be your guide, then. I trust you will find that the lower depths are interesting.'

Johnston didn't. He followed the silent guide for some time, but found little to bolster his disappointment. Narrow corridors and glossy panelling had replaced the wide streets and towering edifices of ground level — but it remained the city, even here. He had nursed the tiny hope that perhaps in the depths of the world he might discover rock and earth and soil in their natural condition. But there was nothing. Only the everpresent product of man's industrial genius. And behind the walls thrummed the energy of the mighty machines that made possible the existence of the miles of city overhead.

He turned around, defeated. 'I think I'll go back.'

'Very good, sir.'

A sudden thought occurred to Johnston. 'How far down are we?'

'Twenty-seven miles.'

He repeated the figure to himself. 'Is this the lowest level?'

'If you mean, does the city extend below us, no, it does not, sir.'

Mr Johnston stopped and tapped the floor with the toe of one shoe.

'Then what's down there?'

'Several miles of insulatory material.'

'And after that.'

'Hell, sir.'

'*Hell*?'

'An archaic term that describes the inner core of the planet. That is all. There is . . . nothing more.'

Mr Johnston stared down at the floor, trying to picture the elemental fury of the molten core of the raped planet. And he smiled. Ever so faintly.

It was something to know that man had never been clever

enough or proud enough to master the molten fury of the world's core.

The guide saw him aboard the elevator and waited for the door to slide shut. When he saw the lift was safely ascending he crossed the passageway and wedged himself upright in a narrow niche carved into the wall. As soon as his shoulders made contact with a particular strip of metal a beam of ions lashed through his chest and deactivated him.

His eyes glazed over and he stared emptily into a soulless darkness.

Johnston's first thought upon reaching the surface was to hire an air-car and sweep the air above the city until he found what he was looking for. Perhaps from such a high vantage point he might yet see where the city ended and what lay beyond. But what if the city was interminable? That would mean that anything real could only exist in tiny, hidden places that could easily be overlooked in his haste. He had no idea what he was looking for or what he might find. It might be something as tremendous as a ragged mountain range or something as fragile as a single flower blossoming between the towering cliffs of the city's blocks.

He would have to walk. Scour the city on foot. Journey to the limits of the megapolis and beyond. He had plenty of time, so what matter if it took him months or years to find what he was looking for? It was something he *had* to have. Against that tremendous desire time ceased to have relevance.

He began his quest the following morning.

He travelled light. There was no need to burden himself with anything other than the clothes he wore. The city would take care of him. That was what it was there for.

He strode out when the early light of morning was jesting with the almost invisible ramparts of the city and the pavements at street level were deserted and still lit by the ghostly neons. The sullen walls regarded his progress with disdain and then stared glumly towards the eternally bare sky.

He wore a compass strapped around one wrist. That was

to enable him to keep a constant northwards course. He had no wish to revolve in circles. And his eyes were bright with the fires of adventure.

By midday his enthusiasm had diminished. His legs ached and he felt peculiarly light-headed. He sat down on the edge of the pavement and let the frantic bustle of the city move around him. Overhead, air-cars whispered silently through their lanes. People and robots made meagre use of the pavements; most of them preferred the speed and hygiene of the subterranean commuters to actual physical movement along the once crowded streets.

A while later he got up and resumed his journey. The eagerness had faded from his step and now he looked forward resolutely to a long, painful ordeal for the next few days. After that he hoped his legs would become accustomed to the unfamiliar exercise.

By dusk he had covered a distance of perhaps nine miles. The city remained unchanged. The gaunt ramparts still glared dispassionately down upon his insignificant figure.

He was again alone on a deserted street. The blank-faced people of the earth had descended to their burrows.

Where he must soon follow. His body was one fiery, intolerable ache. More than anything else in the world he needed rest.

He found a hostelry and booked in for the evening.

In the morning he arose, refreshed, and resumed his patient journey.

So the days passed. Five of them. In that time he lost count of the miles he had journeyed northwards and still there was no sign of a break in the stifling atmosphere of the megapolis. He had explored a hundred different streets and byways, only to be rewarded with the familiar featureless walls of interminable buildings. There did seem no end to his prison.

He began stopping people in the streets and asking them a question.

'Excuse me, but have you seen anything *real*?'

Blank, sad-happy eyes would stare back at him. Some would say, 'Seen *what*?'

And Mr Johnston would explain, excitedly, 'I thought you might know of a place somewhere in the city where there are things that are real and not...you know, *made*. Trees and flowers and that sort of thing.'

Many times only incredulous disbelief would be his answer.

'What are you talking about, you there? Something that hasn't been *made*? No make sense, man. Better see your psych . . . .'

And they would hurry off.

Others didn't even bother to answer him but shook their heads and went on their way, embarrassed by his question.

What was the use, he wondered. If human beings had forgotten the concept of what something real was, then how would he ever find what he was looking for?

So he didn't ask any more, but continued northwards, wandering aimlessly and disillusioned towards he knew not what.

When dusk came that evening he continued walking. He resented the night and the fatigue it brought. He wanted to make use of every possible hour in the hope that each step was bringing him a little closer to his precious goal.

But he pushed his weary body too much. The world around him dissolved into a whirling blur and he flung out his hands suddenly to keep from toppling over.

In vain. He collapsed into an unconscious heap upon the pavement. Night buried him and the neons bathed his body gently with a friendly radiance.

A while later an air-car came cruising along and hovered beside him. A door opened and two men stepped out on to the concrete. Together they lifted Johnston into their vehicle.

Their handling brought him back to a semi-conscious state. He looked up into two curious, intelligent eyes.

'Your name?' The question was brisk and to the point.

'Johnston,' he said, 'Harry Johnston.'

'Are you a resident of this district or a transient?'

He thought the matter over for a moment. 'Transient, I suppose. Traveller, really. You see, I'm looking for something real.'

The eyes didn't even flicker. 'How far are you going?'

'As far as I can. But it's so . . . slow. So slow . . .'

The face before him frowned. 'You've been . . . *walking*?'

Mr Johnston nodded. He was wide awake now.

'Then I suggest you hire an air-car. There's an agency in Block 10789. You can go there first thing in the morning. In the meantime, we're taking you to a hostelry for the evening. I think you'll find it more comfortable than the sidewalk.'

The following morning he took the patrolman's advice and hired an air-car. There was no harm in trying, he figured. And besides—six days of fruitless walking had all but beaten him. An ascent skywards might at least provide him with the widest possible view of his environment.

But he feared the discovery it might bring. Perhaps that was the real reason why he had kept putting it off for so long.

As the car shot skywards his fears took substance. He looked down at the miles of city unwinding beneath him and felt a great shaft of despair sink deep into his heart. There did indeed seem to be no end to it. It stretched out all around him and swept up against the horizon in ragged, bitter ramparts.

The maximum altitude of the air-car was only a few thousand feet. There was nothing for him to do but proceed morosely northwards across the unfriendly mantle of the megapolis.

The hours accumulated like drops of sweat upon his forehead and then, miraculously, he perceived a gradual tapering off to the city's rooftops. The great monster was gradually lowering the height of its mantle. Towering blocks gave way to smaller units. He followed the pattern farther until the buildings ceased to grasp at his little vehicle and contented themselves by slumbering closer to the surface of the world.

The air-car sped out across the incredible diminished city. Behind him rose the central nucleus, forming a gigantic barrier against the sunlight.

It was almost as if he had travelled through some immense mountain range and was now wandering, a little dazed, through the rolling foothills. The intense concentration of buildings and roadways had given way to wide, almost deserted avenues of glass and concrete. Johnston stared down happily and pushed his carriage to maximum speed. This was the first time he found any alteration in the apparently inevitable pattern of the city. The thought of what lay ahead of him sent his heart thumping excitedly.

Too soon. Another hour saw a grotesque shape lumbering up from the horizon, until the familiar shape of yet *another* city began to grow before him. His elation was swallowed by the everpresent despair. And dimly, or was it only in his imagination, he perceived beyond it the ghostly shape of still another city. And beyond it another and another and another. Erupting from the metal sheath that encompassed the planet like monstrous boils.

He punched a button on the dash. 'Maximum altitude,' he snapped.

The car hesitated and then shot skywards.

At fifteen thousand feet he looked down at the world spread beneath him and cursed angrily at the voracious little biped that had made it so. For now, indeed, there did seem no end to it. A world encased by a succession of gigantic cities, each one connected by the slumbering suburbs that spread between them like a mottled tablecloth. And nowhere was there a break in the terrible carapace. No lakes, no rivers, no trees, no birds. Nor was there a cloud in all the sterile sky.

He let the car spiral towards the rooftops, idling through an atmosphere where every season was but a mild summer and every current of air predictable, until the brilliance of an unclouded sunset brought the filters automatically across the windows.

From a spot far to the west a sudden difference became apparent. A colour jumped up from the horizon and beguiled his memory.

While the air-car continued his descent he puzzled over the strange hue. There was something *different* about it.

How different?

Why, because it was *green*. And not a shade he was accustomed to. Not at all like the drab and harsh colours that infected the cities. Much more subtle. As if it was a composite of many varied but similar hues. The colour one expected to find in, oh, trees and gardens, where each growth possessed its own personal variation of the general shade, and where . . . .

He swung the air-car in a sharp turn and accelerated towards the west. Swept across the motionless ocean of steel. And gradually the almost imperceptible smudge of impossible green blossomed and grew across his range of view, until he was staring with unbelieving eyes at the grandeur swelling up before him.

Abruptly, the Great Park exploded across his eyes. He recoiled from the assault of greenery that filled his world, and punched the descent button eagerly.

The tiny vehicle spiralled down and came to rest upon a richly carpeted lawn in the middle of the Great Park.

Mr Johnston sat there, unmoving, blinking his eyes and telling himself that it wasn't a dream and that such a place really existed in the world, after all.

A park. A gigantic park. And he had thought that man had forgotten.

How could any man forget such beauty as this?

He stumbled through the doorway and stood a little unsteadily beside the air-car. His eyes swung down and marvelled at the manner in which his feet sank into the soft, green grass. And all around him was a silence so incredibly still and satisfying that he began to doubt the sanity of it all.

Green hills rolled away into the distance. Trees dotted and sometimes dominated the landscape. And there was a sense of timelessness hanging over the great land that rendered the cities to some great limbo.

And indeed, there was no sign of them here. Tall as they were, the park was so placed and recessed so as to render them invisible. Johnston could well have been alone in his own private world.

Never had he imagined such a prize.

Paradise. And if not, as close to it as he could wish. What strange quirk of human nature had presaged the isolation of this oasis from the rest of the world? Perhaps he had been a little too quick in his bitter judgment of his fellow men.

But why hadn't the Controller told him of such a place? His brief puzzlement disappeared when he recalled his own impatience. If he had gone on to Room 12 as directed he would no doubt have been directed to the park—and have saved himself several long, wearying days of trekking. Still, there was no denying the fact that privation heightened pleasure. He would never have been able to experience the blissful fulfilment he now felt if he had been calmly ushered off from the city to this idyllic refuge.

He left the air-car and wandered slowly across the grass to where a cobbled pathway wound up through the trees. He followed the stones for some distance until the vehicle was hidden behind a small rise and the last contact with the city world vanished. He was alone in Eden.

As he walked he left the path occasionally to take a closer look at the different species of trees and shrubs growing at carefully spaced intervals, each with a descriptive name plate attached to a trunk or imbedded in the soil. The words were incomprehensible to him. Most of them had long since vanished from the world's vocabulary. But just the same he smiled and nodded his head as if he understood what the plaques said, and moved on the next one.

142

The pathway seemed determined to wind on indefinitely through the trees. After a while he wearied of walking and sat down upon the unfamiliar grass. Long slanting rays from the setting sun sent shadows racing across the landscape. Wondrous perfumes rose up from the ground around him. A sudden desire swept down upon him and he sprawled out full length upon the grass, one hand flung indolently across his eyes to shield them against the sunlight.

He swam lazily in the waters of fulfilment. All his resentment crumbled and he forgot the world he had left behind. He took in a great lungful of the heavily perfumed air and expelled it grudgingly. It was so different from the stale smell of the city air.

He rolled over on to one side and stared into the grass. He studied the tiny slivers of green as if he was investigating some profound secret.

And there was movement in the grass. Fascinated, he watched a long column of ants moving through the miniature jungle, and marvelled at their patience.

A strange sound danced overhead. He looked up and saw a strange creature beating the air with wide appendages and flitting through the dusk to disappear amongst the branches of a nearby tree.

A bird!

It gave another shrill cry and was silent.

Johnston sat up excitedly. There were live creatures in the park! What momentous discoveries had he yet to make? And night was falling rapidly now. He didn't have much time.

He scrambled to his feet and hurried over the crest of the next hill. Below him the ground dropped away to a small hollow, and rose again towards another crest. But the hollow was the most remarkable thing he had ever seen. It was covered by a broad sheet of water that could only be a lake, and upon the placid surface several strange creatures sat with their long necks arched indolently towards their reflections.

In his haste to get down the hill he stumbled and rolled the last few yards. But he got up laughing with the sheer joy of existing. Then he approached the edge of the lake and stared, wide-eyed, at the impossible creatures now condescending to take notice of him.

He watched them for a long time and then, when the stars began to break out like an impatient rash upon the fading face of day, he lay down on the grass by the water's edge and marvelled at the way his park became transformed by the magic of starlight.

Later, he fell asleep. The air was pleasantly warm and he had no thought of dangers. His last conscious thought was that his journey of discovery had only just begun.

He awoke to a green morning, the first he could ever remember. He bathed his face in the cool waters of the lake and then bade goodbye to the indolent swans. There was another hill he had yet to surmount.

He left the lake below him and passed over the crest of the next rise. And he was unprepared for the splendour that opened at his feet. Instead of the familiar, all-conquering green he had become accustomed to, the country below him erupted into dazzling colour. Mile after mile of gaudy and subtle hues stretched before him, where even the horizon was a bewildering explosion of flowers.

So great was the onslaught of colour that it made him dizzy. And he descended the pathway like a man in a dream. Long colonnades of beautifully landscaped gardens beckoned his step. He began to wonder if he was really dreaming it all. So much beauty had no right to exist in his world. And yet, the roses were real enough to his touch. The fragrance they poured forth would have intoxicated a Controller and would have been capable of shattering any false dream. And then there came the incredible splendour of the orchids, remarkably resplendent with life in such a temperate climate. And there was more. Much more. Mile after mile of exotic blooms. A veritable forest of flowers stretching for as far as the eye could see.

But who looked after all this, he wondered. And who tended the lawns and trees and fields?

He was still puzzling over this annoying little detail when he came upon the Caretaker's house.

He stood quite still on the edge of the small clearing and studied the peculiar building on the other side. It was only a small construction, and seemed to have been made from the same material as the trunks of the trees surrounding it. Wood, or something like that, he remembered, proud of his latent memory. He had never seen wood before. It seemed impossible that some still existed in the world of the cities.

And it quite surprised him. He had been thinking along the lines of a vast army of robots marching backwards and forwards across the endless lawns and keeping watch over the blossoming of the roses. He had never imagined that the Great Park was cared for by a little old man sitting alone in the centre of everything in a small house carved from the very wood of the trees.

He knocked uncertainly on the door.

'Come in,' answered a patient, tired voice.

Mr Johnston opened the door.

The room inside was lit only by the sunlight filtering in through a number of uncurtained windows. The furniture was incredibly archaic and also fashioned from wood.

The old man was sitting near a window in the far corner. He nodded to Johnston and motioned him to close the door behind him and sit down.

'You've come to see my park,' the old man said, in a voice that could quite easily have been compounded of wood as well. The words were a statement, not a question.

Johnston said, 'That's right. I . . . I had no idea that such a place existed. I thought that it was...all gone. That the cities had swallowed everything.'

'No, not everything is "gone",' the old man said, softly. Johnston thought that he had never seen anybody look quite so old. Ancient, really. As if he had been sitting here like this for...centuries. 'Some places remain. Parklands, like this estate. But not many people come to them any more.'

'Why not?' To Johnston it was inconceivable that people should want to stay in the cities when beauty such as this existed on their very doorstep. He said as much to the old man.

The Caretaker nodded his white head, sadly. 'What you do not understand, Mr Johnston, is that most people have forgotten what beauty is. And the rest...can't be bothered.'

That made sense. It wasn't only that a percentage of humanity had been replaced by machines that moved and looked and acted almost like human beings, but that the remainder of the people had assumed the manner of the machines. Their personalities had been swallowed up by the bare, mechanized world around them until they were almost indistinguishable from the robots. A sterile environment had moulded their thinking into equally barren channels. And that was why it was so difficult to separate man from machine.

'You're the first visitor I've had in...years', the old man said. In a voice heavy with time.

The subtle pause that separated the last word from the rest of the sentence was lost upon Johnston. His mind buzzed busily with urgent questions.

'But surely you don't look after all *this* yourself?'

'Heavens no, young man. There are...robots,'—he used the word with obvious reluctance—'machines to tend the gardens and the lawns. I am too old to do anything but sit and wait.'

'But I didn't see any—'

'Of course you didn't. They do their necessary work by night. Senses such as theirs have no need of the light of day. It prevents them from despoiling the landscape when visitors arrive. Not that it would make much difference these days.'

Johnston thanked the commonsense that had prompted such a decision so long ago. He couldn't bear the thought of the sight of a machine trundling over his park. By now it had become *his* park—his and the old man's.

'Do you live here, all alone?'

The old man shrugged. 'Where else? I have no need of the cities. The cities have no need for me. Here I can be as one with nature. I am fed and looked after by...by the machines. A necessary evil, I'm afraid. My life is complete, I wish for no more.'

To Johnston it began to sound more and more like Paradise. 'I'd like to stay here. With you,' he blurted out, passionately.

The old man frowned, uneasily. 'I doubt if that would be possible. The city—'

'To hell with the city! It doesn't care what happens to me. What difference does one life here or there matter?'

'On the contrary, a great deal. You must remember Mr Johnston, that you represent part of an equation. A monstrous equation that enables the city cybers to keep the world functioning smoothly. You are part of a vast, complex system of automation where every act is predictable and measured against the consequences of a billion others. To remove you would introduce a random factor into the calculations that could easily endanger the successful management of the city and, ultimately, the entire world. No, I'm afraid that you won't be able to stay. But you may visit often.'

'But what if I apply for permission?' Johnston pressed. 'They couldn't refuse, could they? I mean, what does it matter, either way?'

The old man was silent for a moment. Then he said: 'I suppose they might consider it. It would certainly bear investigation.'

They both fell silent. Johnston stared out of the window at the garden and listened to the birds punctuating the stillness with their cries.

'How did it all begin?' he wondered, aloud.

The old man looked up. 'How did *what* begin, Mr Johnston?'

'The cities. The world. Everything. When did we start eating our planet?'

'No one knows, my boy. No one. Perhaps it began when the Gods left earth and ascended to the stars. And closed the Gates so we could not follow. And left us here to perpetuate. We had only one world. What else could we do?'

'But where will it *end*?' Mr Johnston said.

'End? But it has ended, hasn't it?'

They stared at each other, unable to answer each other's question.

'Do you think they'll ever come back?' Johnston said.

'Who?'

'The Gods.'

'Who can answer such a question? For all we know they may have already forgotten us.'

Forgotten us.

As we, too, will one day forget them.

The ultimate end of everything, to be lost in the great vaults of memory.

He asked the Caretaker further questions about the Park. How far it extended, what else it contained, and when the old man spoke of wild life and rivers and fish, an impatience suffused his thoughts. Conversation with the old man only brought a return to his despair. He longed to be out in the open air again.

'I think I'll be on my way,' he eventually announced, and got up from the old chair that miraculously had not sundered under his weight. 'There is so much I want to see before nightfall.'

'Certainly. But do call again. It is not very often that I have the opportunity to . . . converse.'

They walked to the door and the old man opened it for him and let in the splendour of nature again.

Already the afternoon was drawing to a close. They must have talked for hours. Or was it only that the days seemed so terribly short now? He seemed to remember them being much longer. But that was a long, long time ago. Man had changed all that, as he had changed everything else.

Except this, he thought. *All this beauty around me. He had sense enough to retain this.*

By the doorway was a tremendous rose bush. Scarlet blooms burst hungrily towards the sunlight. A sudden desire swept over him and he stretched out a hand to pluck one of the flowers to carry with him, next to his heart.

'No.' The cry from the Caretaker shattered the solitude abruptly.

Johnston stayed his hand a scant few inches from the irresistible petals. He looked around at the little old man.

'You must not touch the flowers.'

A sudden anger of resentment flared inside Johnston. He had had enough of orders. They had no place *here*.

Defiantly he curled his fingers carefully around a thorn-free stem of a rose and plucked it quickly from the bush. He held it up in plain view of the Caretaker and sniffed the delicate perfume arrogantly.

In his hand the rose withered and died. Dead leaves crumpled into a wraith-like, gossamer remnant of the texture of a spider's web.

Johnston stared down at his empty hand. And then looked up at the Caretaker. The anguished look of despair in the old man's eyes was the most terrible sight he had ever seen.

Trembling, he knelt down by the bush and got a firm grip upon the base of the plant. The whole splendid thing came away easily. And while it withered and faded away to gossamer fragility he saw the almost invisible tendrils whipping back into the dark soil.

The truth took a while to break over his reluctant knowledge. And with it came the realization that the beautiful roses were only fakes, complex re-creations that, once separated from the field that produced them, became only a miniscule plastic film that could be screwed up in the palm of one hand.

And if so the rose, so the entire garden. The trees, the lawns, the birds—everything. Why had he been foolish enough to believe that such a place had really survived? It was nothing more than an elaborate memorial. Nothing else. A brilliant mock-up of a diversified group of flowers. and trees that could never exist and promulgate under the same identical conditions.

He had been tricked.

A low cry began in the depths of his throat and rose to an anguished scream. 'You filthy liar! And you almost had me believing . . . . Damn you! All I ever wanted was the truth. You could have given it to me. Only you. And you chose to lie, lie . . .!'

His eyes widened suddenly, and then narrowed into angry slits. His fingers curled into angry fists. 'And why? I should have known, should have guessed. Because you're a robot, a bloody machine, like all the others. Aren't you? Aren't you?'

The old man tried desperately to repair the damage. 'I . . . I told you not to pick the rose,' he stammered. 'I tried to stop you from . . . from finding out.'

'From finding out the truth!' Johnston screamed, and he smashed one fist into the old face. The Caretaker staggered back against the wall. Johnston followed him, hammering away with vicious fists, screaming over and over again, 'Machine! Bloody machine!'

The old man fell to the ground. Johnston slammed one foot against his head and kept kicking away at the face until the synthetic fibres appeared through the mashed protoplasm. Then he turned away and ran across the clearing, away from the house and into the long colonnades of flowers.

He began sobbing and tearing away at the bushes, trying desperately to find at least one that was real. But every bloom withered in his hand. Every branch he wrested from a sapling crumbled into nothingness in his hands. He swore and grappled with the wires retreating into the soil. Tore them free and watched them writhe like drunken snakes in his hands. Saw how his furious haste had scratched and ripped at his arms. How the blood began to flow from the cuts.

And he laughed.

There was a whisper of thunder overhead. He flung back his head and looked up at a hovering air-car. There were two men inside studying him dispassionately. The same two men who had picked him up in the city.

Agents of the city. Who had watched him, followed him, let his whim have its way.

Come to take him back. Back to the constricting horror of the city man had made, that encompassed the world in a straitjacket of steel twenty-seven miles thick.

Where nothing real existed and where robots had become so close to humans and humans so close to machines that it was no longer possible to tell one from the other.

'Don't you understand?' he screamed up at them. '*I might be the last man alive!*'

They just looked at him. The air-car began to descend.

Johnston watched it come closer. He knelt amongst the flowers he had once thought real and which now appeared as artificial as the world he had fled. He lowered his head and looked down at the bright spots of blood on his hands.

There was something real. His own blood. It had been there all along. The only thing that distinguished him from the machines. The one mark of man that remained uncopied.

And he made his decision. He would never return to the

city. Better death than intolerable strangulation in that hideous prison.

He tore up a bush and grabbed the writhing tendrils of wire and scraped away savagely at his wrists until the blood gushed redly from the swollen artery.

The air-car lurched and fell the last few yards. The door opened and the two men got out. They approached him cautiously. One of them held a long, narrow instrument that could be a weapon.

Johnston didn't care. He felt weak and dizzy now.

He held his bleeding wrist aloft. 'You see *this*, you damned machines? I can do something you can never do. I can die. *Die*!'

They said nothing, but stood there, a little apart, staring at him. He marvelled at their patience, at their lack of concern, and wondered if they really understood the concept of death.

Only when the blood stopped flowing and the earth had swallowed the last drop of his precious fluid did he comprehend their patience. He stared at his upheld arm and willed the blood to flow afresh. But none gushed forth from the tattered wrist. His veins were empty, already collapsing.

And still he lived. The pulsating awareness buried within his skull had no need of the external carapace designed only to delude his conscience and his fellow men. His was the ultimate evolution. A mind that existed independently of his synthetic body.

There were no tears to express Johnston's grief. His weary body seemed suddenly to split asunder. He sprawled out upon the treacherous earth and, with his face buried in the lying grass, wept for the passing of all things real.

And he never sensed the approach of the watchers nor felt the narrow shaft of ions that entered his chest and cancelled his soulless life.